KNOCK THREE TIMES

**More modern folk tales
for a troubled world...**

This book is part of an ongoing project of the *New Weather Institute*. After decades of campaigning for a better world, our times seem ever-more troubling, standing on the verge of potentially irreversible ecological decline and in the grip of toxic social division. *Knock Three Times* is our third volume of tales following *There was a Knock at the Door,* and *Knock Twice.*

This edition brings together leading experts in climate hazards, earth science, zoology, health, finance, and progressive business together with storytellers, poets, artists and activists. Each contributor works in different ways to make the world a better place and safer from systemic threats, but also sees the limits of simply throwing facts at people in the hope that this will lead to change.

Here they take a different approach and turn to telling stories. Some reveal the unsafe foundations we stand on, others suggest the way ahead. We thank them for their contributions and being willing – in fact enthusiastic – to try something different. These tales are very modern, yet rooted in ancient story telling traditions. We need detailed plans and policies to prevent climate breakdown and build a world where all can thrive. But we also need better stories to first imagine and believe in its possibility. Here are some. We hope you enjoy them. If you haven't before, and are moved to write your own, we would love to hear from you.

Knock Three Times

28 modern folk tales for a troubled world

Edited by Andrew Simms & Bill McGuire

THE REAL PRESS/New Weather Institute
www.therealpress.co.uk/www.newweather.org

Published in 2019 by the Real Press with the New Weather Institute.

www.therealpress.co.uk

ISBN (print) 978-0995662353

ISBN (ebook) 978-0995662360

Contents

"We sense new weather
We are on our marks
We are all in this together"

Carol Ann Duffy

Foreword

We understand the world through the stories we tell and use them to pass insights between generations. The extraordinary challenges faced by this generation need new stories and storytellers to make sense of them. *Knock Three Times* is a collection that does just that. It steps forward boldly, with wit, twists and creativity to reveal threats to our common future, and suggests how they might be overcome.

Caroline Lucas MP

Introduction

"People are suffering. People are dying.
Entire ecosystems are collapsing.
We are in the beginning of a mass
extinction. And all you can talk about
is money and fairytales of eternal
economic growth. How dare you!"
Greta Thunberg, addressing the
United Nations, September 2019

It could be something taken straight from a folk or fairy tale. A young child with a gift for seeing the truth, and the courage to tell it, sails across a great wide ocean to a land with a palace where the most powerful people on earth gather. Fearlessly, she berates them for the suffering their complacency is causing and the perils people face as a result. Then she tells them what to do: act on the science of the climate emergency.

Most powerful of all, and again like something conjured from a firelight story, her impact comes from a complete lack of guile. Her earnest delivery comes unfiltered, straight from the heart. The directness is part of what she calls her 'gift'. Because the Swedish schoolgirl, Greta Thunberg, has Asperger's Syndrome. She describes herself how one consequence of this condition – the difficulty she finds in being with others – contributed to her decision to begin the lone protest which sparked a global movement. Another effect is that she holds herself to very high standards and expects others to do so too. She does not set out to please people or be liked, and is not interested in excuses. The tale continues.

In the summer of 2018, Sweden was suffering record heat waves, it was the hottest summer since the country's records began and wildfires were burning through its forests. Elections were due in September. In the midst of this conflagration, Greta began her solitary protest – *Skolstrejk för Klimatet* (school strike for climate) – outside the Swedish parliament. Soon others joined and the #FridaysforFuture school strikes spread around the world, fuelling other protests like those of Extinction Rebellion.

Greta's approach was coolly logical, she questioned why she should attend school and listen to teachers when politicians weren't listening to the facts. She committed to strike each week until the politicians acted.

It's ironic that the young woman whose recent life carries the contours of a slightly unlikely story, rightly accuses the powerful of believing in 'fairy tales of eternal economic growth'. Of course, she is right. 'Fairy tale' is a synonym for something that cannot exist in the real world. Much the same is true when something is described as being an 'old folk tale' – it is not to be believed. Both types of story, however, aren't meant to be plausible in their worldly details; they are about revealing deeper truths.

There are plenty of myths, fables, folk and fairy tales that warn of the destructive power of greed and of disregarding natural limits. From the Midas touch to the flight of Icarus, King Canute's inability to halt the incoming tide, and the abuse of the goose that laid the golden eggs, there is wisdom embedded in our cultural heritage that could better guide us.

Another function of folk tales, written about in the introductions to our previous story collections – *There was a knock at the door* and *Knock Twice* – is to help people come to terms with extremes of human experience. Tales often have their roots in times of struggle, during wars and the famines that result from them. In the light of our current political and ecological upheavals, and the great displacements of people driven by climate extremes and blocked by intransigent borders, we need new tales more than ever for this reason.

But even greater, as the forms of an old culture of unbounded consumerism die, we need new stories to help us imagine and make the rapid transition to a different future. 'Stories are one of the most ancient and most effective ways of making sense of the world,' wrote the author Philip Pullman in a foreword to the first collection of stories in this series, adding: 'When we try to live a good life in a world we seem to be simultaneously destroying, there is nothing more valuable or worth encouraging."

In this regard, nothing has changed since our last collection. In other, very important ways, many things have. Partly because of the real life tale of a Swedish child with a very special gift, the world is dramatically more aware of the critical threats to the biosphere and our life support systems. Millions are taking to the streets and taking risks to push for change from below, because those on high have failed to act on the science.

There are too many rich tales here to pick out any one, but we can guarantee you a rich and surprising variety. All, in different ways, seek to reveal a truth or light the way ahead. We invite you to knock three times on this book, turn the page, and begin a journey that may contain some peril, some surprises and doors that may open, hopefully, to new possibilities. Although to sometimes highly differing degrees, this is the prospect and predicament facing us all.

Andrew Simms & Bill McGuire

1
The Boy with Four Ears
Sarah Deco

Once there was a boy who was born with four ears. Two were just like yours and mine, the ones that fan out like shells on the side of your head. But inside those, deep inside, there was another pair. They moved, furling and unfurling like roses or sea anemones and could sense quite different sounds.

This boy whose name was Michael could hear, as he lay in his pram, the wind singing its wide weary song, as it carried pollen across the park. He could hear the high ringing tones of the grass. As he became a little older and began to understand language, he understood that the wind and the grass, the trees and even the sun sang songs, containing language. Not words exactly, but they sang, and it meant something, to him at least.

'We are here... ' they sang, 'we are with you... we are always alongside you.'

When he heard these songs, he felt joyful and safe.

As he grew a little older, he discovered snails sang a slow squeaking song, the ash tree in the garden had a particular deep and sonorous voice. The daisies in the grass had their song, the ants and the worms had theirs. His mother would often look at him as he listened.

'Look at Michael' she would say. 'What is he listening to, do you think?' His father and brother would shake their heads and laugh.

When he went to school the teacher said,

'Pay attention, Michael. Look at me! Stop gazing out of the window.'

Little by little the rosebuds of ear folded in their petals. Michael no longer heard the grass singing.

Michael grew up and left school, he spent long days in the park, feeling sad. His ears nearly opened again once, a few petals unfurled as he sat one day by the pond watching a heron standing on a rock sticking out of the water like an old sage contemplating fate.

'We are here', said the trees... 'We are here with you', said the wind...

But Michael was too busy being sad to really hear them.

His mother said he really must get a job. So, he worked in the multi-coloured daze of lights in the local shopping centre hanging and re-hanging clothes that shoppers had dropped on the floor. The music was very loud.

After a year or two of that, he got a place in a big shiny college that trained people to go 'into business'. His mother was very pleased. He got a job in a company that laid concrete over grass and cut down trees. He did well. He earned money. He got married and had children of his own.

He had a daughter and two sons. His daughter had four ears, but his sons had only two.

He saw his daughter listening with the same expression he had worn when he was that age, it made him sad at first and then angry, as he saw her ears close too. He didn't know how to help her.

His daughter grew up to be sad most of the time, as her ears closed so her joy shut down. She went to doctors, to clinics, she was given drugs. It was now as if she could hear hardly anything at all.

Michael grew old and was taken from the hospital to a hospice. As he lay looking out at the tops of the trees waiving in the breeze, a nurse opened a window. His inner ears quivered and came to life again, their petals shook and stretched.

'We are here', said the trees... 'We are here,' said the wind and the clouds... 'We were here all the time.'

2
No Apples for the Pig
Jan Dean

They were supposed to share the apples:

One for you,
One for me,
One for the pig in forest and field
And one to give back to the tree.

That was how it worked. Everybody knew that. But then it changed.

No apples for the pig. Pigs can manage very well without apples.

That was a pity, because the pig liked apples and though we all knew that one day we would eat the pig why shouldn't it enjoy an apple in the meantime? Well that brought out a hard stare and a louder voice. *No apples for the pig.*

So then it was:

One for you,
Two for me,
And one shiny apple
To give back to the tree.

Pretty soon no-one remembered that the pig had ever been given an apple. No-one remembered how the pig used to rub against the tree and snout in the earth around it. But we had apples still and every year we shared them. But then it changed.

An apple for the tree? That's just silly. Trees don't need apples. They *make* apples. So no-one laid an apple on the ground by the tree roots. No-one dug a hole and tucked it tight in the space between the roots. That was a pity too, because a thank-you is no bad thing. And feeding what feeds us is right and proper. Well, that brought out a hard stare and a louder voice. *No apples for the tree.* So then it was:

One for you,
Three for me,
Shiny apples from the tree.

Pretty soon, no-one remembered that the tree had ever been included in the sharing at all. And then came the lean year, the mean year, when there were scarcely any apples at all.

Why so few apples? Because it's not a glut year – everybody knows that. Though it was hard to remember when the last glut year had been and the tree looked sort of *thinner*, sort of *sadder*, than it used to, and the soil it grew from was greyer. It misses the pig, it misses the rooting and snuffling. It misses the muck that used to make the earth rich and dark. It misses the seep of juice from the apples we gave back to it. So then it was:

Three for me.

I'm used to three. And you, well, you only ever had one. You won't miss one.

So away you go. Empty. And we won't have a song or a rhyme to remind us. Because sharing is what I say it is. And you remembering just gets in my way.

3
As if by Magic
Kate Potts

Once, in a land not far from here, there lived a woman named Clare. Clare worked in an ordinary office and lived in an ordinary flat. Every day, she would wake at 6am and go downstairs to swim 42 lengths of the long, blue-green ozone pool in her building's basement.

At this hour, she was usually alone in the water – accompanied by the glazed stare of Nola, the life guard. The only sound was the splash of Clare's arms slicing and pummelling the soft water, propelling her body forward. Each morning, Clare fitted in a five-minute pep chat as she ate her muesli. 'Clare, you have so much untapped potential,' said the voice from her tablet (female, well educated, clear as faceted crystal). 'We need to think about how we can maximise this, really turn it to your advantage. Let's talk about how you're using your time.'

Bloom, the wellness company Clare worked for, specialised in motivational coaching and life enhancement. The app created personalised advice, while also pushing products from Bloom's partners, like breathe.com and Karma co-op. Using the implant in Clare's left wrist, combined with her online and banking data, Bloom could schedule Clare's morning swim, order her groceries, choose music that suited her mood. In her day job, Clare tested and tweaked the programming of Bloom's chatbots and their chat scripts to make them warmer and more human-like.

Each day after breakfast, Clare would shower, dress, and head to the office on the 7.30 shuttle bus. The shuttle always appeared the moment she exited the building's steel and glass doors and stepped into the sleeping street. At the office, Clare would meet with her pro-team for a morning update and then sit at her desk to look through the chat log reports and customer feedback.

On a typical day, Clare would have meetings with the marketing team, Bloom's partner companies, and the creative team – as well as writing and tweaking the all-important scripts. Clare knew she wasn't what the company called 'a bright spark', but she made sure she was competent and dependable, and a good listener. Clare took pride in being a stickler for detail; she conscientiously softened the harder edges of the chatbot algorithms, making sure they chirped welcoming phrases and affirmations: 'How are you in yourself?' 'What can Bloom do for you today?'. Colleagues found the rural lilt of Clare's voice and the calm of her loam-grey eyes reassuring.

At lunchtime, she would eat a salad at her desk while reading the news headlines and chatting with her colleague Rowan about the latest serial on Netbox. 'I can't even bear it,' he'd moan, gesticulating between sips of flat white. 'How do they expect me to wait a week for the next episode? I need to know what happens *now*.'

After work, Clare usually went to one of Bloom's scheduled Blossom and Grow sessions. This autumn, she had been learning to speak Spanish with a wiry, exacting woman named Maria. Once every two weeks, Clare would go on a date selected by Bloom's partner app, Bless – usually at one of the newer restaurants in the city centre where she could woozily lose her own reflection, and her date's, in the prisms of glass and chrome, and enjoy small plates of honey-glazed squid, chipotle olives, and bread as light and gauzy as the clouds that hovered in the corners of the bald sky.

Afterwards, there might be a boozy kiss, or even an hour or so of cheery, energetic sex in Clare's enormous white bed. To make the most of her personal growth plan, Clare made good use of Bloom's pro-concierge service, 'As if by magic'. Each Monday morning, a cardboard box of pre-prepped, selected ingredients appeared on her doorstep ready for her to produce her own, carefully balanced meals. Every Saturday morning, a tissue paper package of clean, sweet-smelling laundry appeared on the kitchen table. Her apartment, when she arrived home at night, was always pleasantly tidy and dust-free – though there was only a faint smell of peonies, and never an aggressive odour of cleaning products hanging in the air.

In the morning, there was coffee, cereal, and almond milk in the kitchen, just where she needed it.

The bathroom was stocked with chic cosmetics that smelled of rosemary and lavender. Often, products arrived at the flat before even realised she wanted them: for example, a multi-pack of sports socks, a lipstick, and a bottle of vitamins.

Although Clare worked very hard at Bloom, everything in her life was always pleasingly well-planned and accounted for. She had all but forgotten the chaotic times before – hazy times of scuzzy rented rooms, junk food, scraping by on freelance scraps of work like a dishevelled ghost, times when she had not been focused on her own flourishing.

But there was, as there so often is, a tiny flaw in the beautiful design of Clare's life. It had begun as a chink, a hint, like a swathe of spotted blue mould, an ancient crust hidden in a skirting board.

It all began with a crumb. One Tuesday morning, as she stood in her kitchen space about to spoon crisp flakes, nuts, and dried papaya into a white bowl, she'd noticed a crumb next to the fresh-ground coffee. It was not a familiar crumb. It was a yellow, oily crumb. It didn't match the food she'd eaten there last night: it wasn't a crisp, brown crumb that might have come from the ginger tuille she'd eaten with raspberry sorbet. As she prodded it with the tip of her finger she'd felt revulsion, and then, with surprise, a surge of anger. How dare someone leave their greasy food in *her* flat? How dare they dirty her clean, polished beech kitchen surface? This was an invasion, an outrage.

And then, slowly, she began to picture pro-concierge's 'As if by magic' service not as the automated miracle she'd somehow come to imagine it to be, but as the work of a series of grubby little fairies: real, grotesque bodies, fleshy beings walking right through her space with their sweaty, hobbled feet and staring eyes, scuttling and hiding from her sight, clutching her food, her laundry, her muesli, with their paunchy, grabbing hands. If they ate at her marble kitchen worktop then what else was possible? Were they frying donuts on her stove, shitting in her bathroom, napping in her beautiful bed? Were their skin cells mingling with hers and layering as dust in unkempt corners?

It was unbearable. But, of course, once Clare reported the error to Bloom the malfunction was illuminated and there were no more crumbs to be seen. And yet. In Clare's heavy sleep phase, even while a pre-recorded soundtrack of Atlantic beach washed through her sleeping mind, she felt a creeping sense of wrongness, a kind of nausea, a niggling pain. In the deep and forested corners of her sleep, she heard *their* voices – the invisible ones – as if overhearing a muffled conversation in the next room.

The sound was guttural and soft, like a horse's low whinny, and seemed to her to be barely human. Its low ring and chime resonated in a long-forgotten place, deep underneath her ribs. Sometimes she woke doubled over and sobbing into her white bedlinen, floored by a pain so strong and old she could not fathom it.

Sometimes, there were other traces in Clare's dreams: a long, dark hair in her butternut squash soup, an acrid waft of stale sweat seeping from the pipes beneath her kitchen sink. Sometimes the outlines or edges of these invisible beings appeared as she dreamed – the swish of coat-edge in a hallway, or a glimpse of a body temporarily suggested by an empty dressing gown.

Today, Clare was feeling unaccountably tired. There was a dull ache behind her eyes, and she struggled to keep them open. But her sleep data showed 115 minutes of deep sleep, and 7.8 hours overall, hardly a deficit. There had been gentle rain and bamboo audio last night. She had watched a nature documentary about whales before bed. But her knees ached; she felt as if she'd been overusing the treadmill in her basement gym.

Mid-afternoon, as her head nodded towards the keyboard, Grayson Cullers appeared beside her desk. Grayson was her floor's resident health advisor. He wore a pale green linen suit, a classy approximation, Clare thought, of hospital slacks. His skin was weathered to the point of softness, like expensive leather. 'How *are* you, Clare?' he said, cocking his head slightly to one side, ready to listen.

'Hi Grayson. Yes, fine thanks. A bit tired. How are you?'

'Oh, you know me. Busy with the kids as ever. I've been practicing the new karma co-op regime: cold showers, cyclical breathing. Seems to be doing the job.' Here, Grayson clenched his right fist and thumped his chest firmly, twice, as if demonstrating its solidity. 'How are *you*, Clare?'

Clare blinked. Hadn't he asked her already?

'I'm fine, thanks Grayson. Just, you know, a bit tired.'

'Listen,' said Grayson, stuffing one hand into a bulbous pocket, 'I was wondering if you'd be interested in taking part in a pilot study for us. Nothing heavy; just some new vitamins we've been investigating. Fatigue, waning productivity. That sort of thing.'

'Waning productivity? I don't think I... ' Clare's mouth was mealy and dry. 'I mean, I think my stats are good, Grayson. There's been no fall off. We're experimenting with a new, higher level for pro-empathy response.' Clare had been testing the new, modified scripts with volunteers all week.

'Of course, Clare.' Grayson smiled gently with his eyes. 'The top team are all very happy with your work. But remember, productivity is not just about your life in the office. We're also concerned for your personal growth, your whole-person development. And your life as a team player at Bloom.'

Clare felt herself stymying the warmth of a blush. She looked, involuntarily, towards the blue implant on her wrist, dull and passive as a tattoo. What did it know about her dreams? Could Grayson see some shadow of them in the data? The dread, the almost-presence of those invisible bodies that hovered, taunting at the edges of her sleep? She turned back to see him still smiling, serene, with his eyes. From the bulbous pocket he drew out a small, brown paper package.

She turned it over in her hands. 'Clare Merrigan. One tablet a day, with food' printed there in neat black letters. Now she smiled back, and the bruised feeling behind her eyes seemed to lift a little. 'Thank you,' she said.

'No problem. We're getting good results, but they sometimes take a few days to work. Have patience.'

With that, Grayson was gone. In the envelope, Clare found a shiny silver blister pack of seven pills. She already took a bespoke, targeted multivitamin. She wondered what these could be. Magnesium? Some sort of new iron formulation? For the following few days, Clare swallowed a tablet every morning with her green tea at breakfast, after her swim. They were oval shaped and luminous green, as if made from compacted algae.

She noticed, as Grayson had predicted, very little effect – though perhaps she slept a little more soundly, and the taint of her dreams was easier to bear. On the sixth day, which was a Saturday, she woke to an unusual smell. It segued into her sleep, stronger than the usual fresh, synthesised meadow scent of laundered sheets. It was strangely familiar though. A distant scent of frying dough, sweet and pervasive. Where was it coming from? She remembered, suddenly, something about a fairground, her hand tiny, sweaty and hot in her mother's red, worn palm.

It was 7.30am. Still early, for a weekend. Today she would take a yoga class at the downstairs gym and have brunch at the park café, before getting a head start on the chat script trial stats for next week's presentation. Clare sat up, and yawned. There was something off in her vision, she noticed. Perhaps a new short-sightedness. She'd have to get her eyes tested again. She held up a hand in front of her face. The skin blurred, somehow, at the edges, beginning to wane into the background.

She pinched the back of her left hand; she seemed to be awake, though she couldn't be sure. In the kitchen, Clare switched on the news and watched the weather alerts. She made a large mug of decaf coffee, peeled and ate a perfectly ripe banana. She sat at her table and activated the tablet. Bloom's logo faded into view, with its bright globe of geometric flowers. And then: nothing. No greeting.

'Hello? Hello?' Clare moved her mouth closer to the tablet and spoke directly into it. There was some sort of malfunction. The screen was a deep, empty blue now, no sign of the usual zig-zag graphics measuring her voice and its modulations, no chatbot transcript. No response. 'Hello?'

Clare raised her hands to her face. On the inside of her left wrist, the blue circle of her implant seemed to have hardened and shrunk. She stabbed, agitated, at the tablet, but the screen had frozen. She dug out her phone from her bag and scrolled through for the Bloom helpline number. The recorded voice that answered was warm and kind: 'To speak to a real-time assistant, please press 9'.

Clare waited, listening to the regular thudding of her own heart, as the hold music played on. Then; 'You're through to Denise. How may I help you?' 'Hello. This is Clare Merrigan. Bloom19264. I think there's some sort of malfunction with... ' 'Hello? Who is this? Please state your name and ID.' 'This is Clare Merrigan. Bloom19264. I'm having a problem connecting to the app. Can you let me know –.'

'I'm sorry, but unless you identify yourself, I'm going to have to end the call.' There was irritation, and some anxiety, at the edge of the woman's voice, though she was doing her best to disguise it. 'This is Clare Merrigan.' Clare was almost barking now, despite herself. There was some sort of serious malfunction. Before the helpline assistant could speak again, Clare hung up and placed the phone firmly face down on the table. Quickly, she washed, put on her yoga outfit, and packed her sports bag. She would have to deal with this face to face. In the downstairs lobby, by the lifts, she caught sight of a strange woman she'd never seen before. The woman wore blue overalls, but not the sturdy, fashionable kind. These overalls looked worn and were starting to bag at the knees. There were greyish folds of flesh beneath the woman's eyes. She was carrying a giant, hessian sack. 'What are you doing?' Clare asked.

The woman grunted, glanced up. 'Deliveries', she said.

Clare blinked, and looked again. 'But it's daylight,' she said. 'I can see you. I never see you.'

'You don't?' The woman tilted her head, squinted at Clare with curiosity. 'Would you mind?' she said, taking Clare's left hand as if to shake it politely, then turning Clare's wrist to see the tiny pinhead of a flat blue dot in its centre, next to the bone. She grimaced. 'I think you've been reassigned,' she said.

'Sorry? I've been what?'

'You can see me now because you're a ghoul too.' Clare raised her own left hand to her face and noted, again, its strangely frayed edges, an odd feathering of the flesh. She wanted, suddenly, to be deeply asleep in her bed. Perhaps she still was. 'You can't stay here any more; they won't permit it,' said the delivery woman. As Clare looked at her wrist in front of her, the implant's blue dot wavered and appeared to shrink, almost erasing itself from her body. How would she know when to get up, and when to go to bed, what to eat, and how best to exercise? How could she flourish, with nothing to guide her? She closed her eyes and focused hard on picturing her daily schedule laid out into the distance like a perfectly manicured, geometric garden. There was bile rising inside her, an empty lurch in her stomach.

'You look peaky', the woman said, a matter-of-fact observation. 'You've gone a peculiar colour.' The chaos was a groaning ocean, a thunder of leaping fire.

4
Loch Nowhere
David Boyle

My name is Jeremy Guest and I am writing this deposition in the hope that somehow it will be able to reach my family – though, frankly, I find it hard to believe such a feat will be possible. For reasons you will perhaps understand when you have read it.

It contains a number of events that I would hardly have believed myself had they not happened to me, and even now I doubt myself somewhat. They begin with a barely believable encounter in Scotland, where I happened to be working at the time, attempting to finish a book in the seclusion.

I was staying, you must understand, on the shores of Loch Nevis on the west Highland coast, some way from civilisation. I arrived by boat. In fact, I believe there was then no road there from Mallaig, the nearest town. It was a beautiful spot and I had travelled there alone to finish the book that was behind schedule, tentatively entitled *Twenty-First Century Public Services*. Perhaps its main disadvantage was that it was somewhat damp. Rivers and rivulets poured down the rocks from the hills all around. Every day, even in July and August, it seemed to rain at some point in the day and one was constantly drying one's shoes and clothes next to the fire.

It was a particularly virulent shower that caught me, some way from the house, that afternoon, without an anorak and I struggled to find some shelter. By luck – at least, it seemed so at the time – I was next to a small wooden bridge that crossed one of the powerful waterfalls that speed down into the loch from above. I peered hopefully beneath the bridge, because I would otherwise have been drenched.

My heart leaped a little as I saw a small ledge under there by the fast running water and swung myself under quickly. What did surprise me, however, was that the ledge turned out to be considerably larger than I had imagined. Indeed, it opened out into the darkness and gloom along the side of the stream.

It was immediately clear that I was not alone.

A cheery voice came out of the darkness. It sounded Scottish.

"Hello, welcome my dear sir! I insinuate that you got caught too, did you not?"

"I certainly did," I said. "I didn't see you ahead of me on the path."

"Ah, well," said my companion. "I think I've been here through many of the storms recently."

These had certainly been numerous, so this sentence did not at the time strike me as odd. Though clearly it did later.

"Here!" he said. "I have a couple of spare biscuits if you'd like to share them."

"That's extremely good of you," I said, accepting the proffered gift, though had still not been able to make out the giver with my own eyes.

It seemed strangely rustic, I had to say. "Unusual taste. Sort of health food, I suppose?"

"Ye coulda saye tha'," said my new friend, laughing uproariously. I could hear the rain beating down on the bridge above us. I could hear his Scottish accent too.

It was that this point that my eyes began to get used to our gloomy hiding place, and I have to say I was surprised again. My new friend, it was becoming clear, was some variety of very small person. Perhaps, I suppose, about three feet high, but in proportion like a man. I had believed him to be sitting rather further away. In reality, he was quite close.

I stared, but he didn't appear to notice.

"What is your name, my friend?" he said. "I have other things we might add to the feast before the storm clears, if you should like that?"

"My name?" I said, rather flustered. "Oh, um, Jeremy. I usually try to avoid health food if I can," I said, aware suddenly that this made me sound like a prig.

Then, to my surprise, he pulled out – though I could not see where from – half a packet of Jaffa Cakes. This time, it was my turn to laugh.

"Good lord, you're a surprise a minute," I said, inexplicably relieved. "I should ask your name, since you know mine."

"My name is Idric of the Loch," he said. "What did you expect? Rumplestiltskin?"

"Why would I expect that?" I said, a little confused. "Here, I mustn't eat all your Jaffa Cakes."

I could see now that he was dressed in a kind of long leather coat which appeared in the darkness to be the same colour as he was, a sort of brown, leathery hue. I could not make him out or allocate him to any kind of category.

"Well, should you want to get home once more, you will need to find me again. Is that not so? And now, I see the rain has lifted and I will leave you. Farewell, Jeremy. I hope to see you again."

I watched him jump out of our hiding place with astonishment, since he was considerably more sprightly than I had expected. I realised I had imagined myself conversing with an old man.

For a moment I was too stunned to move, but realised – as I tried to categorise the experience I had just encountered – that he had been correct about the weather. I lay back in my mud cave and I suppose I must have dozed off, because it was clearly much later when I peered out again. The sun was lower in the sky and the temperature was considerably warmer.

I am not a credulous man but I realised, even then, by the state of my clothes, that I had undergone some kind of supernatural experience. The wool garments I had been wearing had rotted in the damp, though luckily most of my clothes were nylon and had survived the trauma of being underground. I had heard stories about fairies of course – who hasn't? – but of course I never actually believed them in the here and now.

Suddenly, of course, I was not so sure.

I clambered out, brushed myself down, noticing with irritation and embarrassment all the mudstains on my underclothes. It really looked as though I had slept there for decades, I joked to myself – little did I know. Then I drew myself up and looked around, absolutely astonished.

The first thing that caught my eye was a huge orange hood next to my bridge. It said 'Hydro energy unit provided by Knoydart Utilities Ltd'. It was as I wondered how I could have missed such a garish installation that I looked further and then I began to be a little scared, I confess.

How had I failed to realise there were so many human habitations along the side of the loch? How had I missed all this activity on the shore – all these boats which were criss-crossing the water, some sailing and some hovering a little over the surface, powered by what I could only describe as a gentle hum as they glided by? Had I slept through the start of some kind of regatta?

I looked up and down the mountainside and realised that every little burn and waterfall had its own yellow or orange canopy. It was then that I understood that I must be having some kind of hallucination. When a dream comes to you complete, in the sense that it appears completely real and you have to give up trying to pinch yourself awake, I wondered whether perhaps my whole holiday had been the hallucination. When had it begun, after all?

I began to be really frightened. Gathering what I could of my rotten clothes, I walked as fast as I could back to the house I had been staying in. As I walked past a range of the homes built along the foothills of the slopes, and becoming increasingly astonished and frightened as I did so, I realised that the sea was also five or six feet higher than I remembered and, by the time I reached the path that should have taken me down to the beach where my lodging was, I knew the truth before I got there. There was the sea. Beyond it and below it, presumably, was my house. And my book, of course.

My illusion – or so I still imagined it – was that I had fallen asleep and dreamed my way forward by some decades, maybe even a century. I have written quite widely about the future and, even if the whole thing emanated from my imagination, I was fascinated by it. I decided to search out someone I could talk to about it.

There was a makeshift pier nearby and I saw a couple walking along it and went down to meet them. They were helpful, and seemed oddly dressed – whoever thought of wearing a ruff and tights?

"I have been away some time. I've been in America," I told them. "Do you, by any chance, have a local historian I could converse with?"

"Man, I know just the guy you want!" he said. "You want Hamish."

"That is excellent. You could possibly direct me and introduce me? I would be eternally grateful."

"Totally," said the man.

Some minutes later, we stood together, knocking at a door. "Hello!" shouted my friend. "I have a visitor for you: this is my uncle, Hamish McAbdul – this is Msr ... um... ?" He gave me a questioning look.

"Guest," I said. I was about to receive my next shock.

"Msr Guest!" he said, waving an arm without getting up. "Come in, come in! Forgive me – my legs have long since stopped operating. You are no relation, I suppose to Jeremy Guest, famous once in these parts?"

"Relation! I *am* him!" I said, with some joy and relief.

To my surprise, my new friend laughed and repeated his invitation to come in, waving his nephew goodbye.

"Strange coincidence that, because, as you may know, there was a time a century ago when someone called the same name as you went missing in peculiar circumstances. That Msr Guest has not been seen since, I fear. In fact, do you see that white column sticking out of the sea about fifty yards from here? No, not that way – near that dhow that's just going by. See it? That was the old Jeremy Guest Memorial set up by his family back in 2021. That's how I know his name. It is still visible sometimes at low tide and so it's familiar to me. I say, whatever is the matter? Come and sit down, human... "

A sense of horror had gripped me as he told me this. My dream – if that is what it was – was fast becoming a nightmare. A whole range of possibilities swam inside my head, each one less pleasant than the last. All I could do, I felt, was to tell the truth as I saw it.

"The thing is" – I could barely speak – "you won't believe this, I fear, but I think it was me. It *was* me. I don't know how, or what kind of dream we are in, but I may have disappeared into this nightmare or this future tense. Please tell me: what year is it?

"The year? It is 2119, human. Come and talk to me, you interest me strangely. As they used to say."

I told him my story, which – as I expected – he didn't really believe, and he told me his. How the seas had risen and the weather had got warmer and how he had come here as a boy, the grandson of refugees from Syria, before the huge rush of population northwards with the changing climate.

"So we survived the great warming, then? I suppose we must have done."

"We survived by taking action. Humanity, I mean. So far, and the planet is still getting hotter, or so I understand, but not nearly so fast. We have also had to survive civil war too but, again, we managed to arrest those on both sides who were pursuing it."

"Civil war? How so?"

"Ah well," said Hamish dismissively. "That is all some time ago now. Back in the 2020s and 40s. It followed the break-up of the UK. It must have been a strange time, though I wasn't there, of course. It led in the end to the imprisonment for sedition of many leading figures who had encouraged armed rebellion to protect the old United Kingdom. These turned out to be the same ones often who had organised the exit of Britain from the old European Union and, before that, had worked hard to prevent any of the necessary changes to prevent us all being overwhelmed by new weather."

"Of course! Brexit! What happened?"

"You don't know? Well, it all turned out to be rather unimportant because the European Union didn't survive long in that state anyway. But by then the damage had been done to our own union. The Scots left. So did Northern Ireland, and so the civil wars began. It was a traumatic period around the time I was born. You can't break up old empires without these kind of emotions emerging."

"How was it resolved? The civil wars, I mean?"

"Well, as you may know – where did you say you were from again? – Europe is now fifty or sixty nations, all independent and yet connected, just as we are here. Scotland is one of the biggest. But we all live under the auspices of the FBI… "

"The FBI?" I said. "The Federal Bureau of In… "

"No no no – the Federation of the British Isles. We're still nominally a monarchy. King George X still reigns. In a sense, anyway."

"So help me out here… ," a little confused. "Which is the nation? Scotland, England or this FBI?"

"All and none!" said Hamish, laughing. "All and none! It is a pattern that most other European nations have copied. As you must know," he said, momentarily forgetting my story, as well he might. "Now can I get you a dram?"

We talked on. Outside, the sun went down, the darkness fell and the only sound that wafted through the windows of my new friend was occasional laughter, the lapping waters and the hum of hydropower.

He told me how battery power had changed the world. How everything, every home, every building, every metre of road, every brick and every window generated energy; how was there was no shortage of energy any more. How this allowed small communities, like the one he lived in, to fend for themselves – and small nations too – in a way that only the big ones had been able to before.

He told me how the functions of energy and money have begun to merge into *monergy*, and how this led to a proliferation – not just of communities – but also of currencies. His neighbours used a whole variety of these for different aspects of their lives. He explained how this had allowed the devolution of power far lower than before and how, generally, this made people more peaceable. Less cross.

"And every month, from the Scottish government, we all get paid enough to get by on – okay in their own Scottish money, which I wouldn't choose myself. It is controversial again now... "

"How so?" I asked.

"There are those who believe basic income prevents us from being more outward looking – it means we have to protect our shores from refugees because we can't afford for them to come. And on the other side, there are those who want us to go back to the good old 20th century, with big armies, massed consumers, huge growth, great wealth. I need hardly say that I am not one of them... "

We talked on, about how change happens in unexpected ways, sometimes despite its defeat, and how it leads on to more change and more demands. It was, I believed, one of the best conversations I have ever had in my life and, by the end of it, my head was absolutely spinning with concepts, some familiar, some completely unfamiliar.

It was almost as if humanity had managed to take the one path possible for survival and had stuck to it. And, in so doing, putting aside lesser issues of identity and nationality, they had managed to claw together a way of life for themselves.

**

I decided I must seek out my home in London to find what was left of my family, and the hope that it might perhaps provide me with a way of returning to them. My new friend Hamish agreed to loan me the international monergy to get the monorail train direct from Mallaig.

The journey took four hours. The rolling stock had been converted from the trains I had known in my own day, which was a little disconcerting.

We shot across the countryside in silence, though my fellow passengers appeared to be happy enough, wired into some kind of screens. We cut our speed as we went through the old demilitarised zone, what I would have known as the Border country. And as we went I have to say I marvelled at the new cities spread out across the moors and valleys, each one – each home it appeared – designed to provide for its own energy and food needs, just as I had seen by the loch.

As we approached every border, the ticket collector went down the train checking passports and permissions from others like me without the necessary automated equipment (Hamish had given me a great deal of advice on this). Through Scotland, Northumbria, Mercia and England and on into the powerful nation known as London.

Yet this was not London that I understood. There seemed to be almost as much traffic as ever, though it was silent and clearly the air in London was certainly fresh. To my great surprise, the city centre was now a huge estuary nearly all the way up towards Kings Cross Station. The old buildings had mainly gone. It was a shock.

I had almost no luggage and I walked to my home down the Euston and Marylebone Road past the missing towers and the new buildings, like the people, designed in what was clearly a trendy Elizabethan style. I wished I had asked Hamish where parliament now was for the FBI. Westminster was under water, or so I gathered.

Paddington was equally unfamiliar. The old towers had gone and had been replaced by the same kind of homesteads that I had seen all the way down from Scotland – small and white and clean somehow, and self-sufficient. My own home, I was relieved to see, was still standing. I knocked on the door and was staggered to find my own wife opening it.

I began suddenly, and fatally, to hope.

"Darling, I'm home!" I said, but she was clearly frightened and tried to push the door shut.

"Sarah," I shouted, desperate now. "It's me! Do you not recognise me?"

By now, I had my foot in the door and had glimpsed what I hoped to see down the hallway. There was the portrait of my wife, painted as a wedding present.

"There's some crazy guy on the other side of this door! Quick – give me a hand!" she was calling to someone.

"Don't do this to me, Sarah!" I shouted. "Look! There's a picture of you staring at me from the end of the hall, where it's always been!"

The door open slowly, revealing the woman I had taken to be my wife.

"Ohmygod!" she said. "You're talking about Sarah, my great grandmother."

**

These are the facts of my predicament. If you read this published anywhere and you have a proposal that I might use to get back to my own time, I would be grateful if you could contact me at +10276 Scot 307 &^%//ahfrg. Thank you so much.

5
The Blame Salesman
Gregory Norminton

Once upon a time, yesterday or tomorrow, there lived a boy who was malcontent. It was not that the boy lacked the necessities of life – food and shelter and company – for his parents loved him and catered to his every need. Yet he had a sour temper. When someone asked him how he felt, he would reply: 'The worse for seeing you', and it relieved some of his gloom to see the expression on that person's face.

If one of his peers asked him over to play, the boy would bring only a scowl and make fun of his playmate's toys.

There are only so many allowances that people will make for a peevish nature, and, as the boy grew, the number of those willing to put up with him dwindled – which served only to deepen the restlessness in his soul.

Why do others hate and shun me, the boy wondered? Why do they seem content with their lives when mine seems barely to have begun? He chewed over these questions in his private moments. In public, he was sullen and reserved.

Then, one day when the boy was in town, he saw an advertisement on a billboard. TAKE CONTROL OF YOUR LIFE, the advertisement said, and DARE TO

BE GREAT. These slogans hovered in speech balloons above a fat, rich, angry face. The boy recognised the face instantly. It belonged to the Blame Salesman.

The boy felt in his pockets for money. His feet took him to the great hall where the Blame Salesman was giving one of his rousing speeches that very afternoon.

There were many other people in the hall. It was hot and there was a rowdy, eager atmosphere. The lights blazed on the platform and the audience cheered as the Blame Salesman strode out.

When the applause subsided, the Blame Salesman began to speak. He told the crowd how numerous they were. He told them how wise they had been to come to hear him today and to ignore the sneering of the haters and the clever people who pretended that he, the Blame Salesman, was selling snake oil. Believe me, he said, I hate snakes, and many people in the audience laughed.

The Blame Salesman rolled his shoulders. 'You people are the best people,' he said. 'You are the *real* people. Not like those fake people. The polished speakers, the so-called experts. The bleeding hearts. The virtue-signallers who look down on you. And let me tell you something. *Those people are to blame.* They are to blame for everything that goes wrong in your life. Every setback, every rejection, every kiss denied you at the end of a meal you paid for with your hard-earned cash. Because those people are happy to take your money, they're happy to take your vote, but they don't care about you. They're laughing at you.

'Believe me, I hear it all the time, that laughter. And that's why you need me. Because nobody else is going to tell you the truth. Everybody else is part of the Lie. The Lie – remember that word – the Lie is everything you've ever been told by your teachers at school, by your snooty neighbour, by the scientist who tells you the world is dying. The Lie is what keeps you in your place, what keeps you quiet.

'Now you noticed that I didn't charge you for coming here today. I won't take a cent off you, not one penny or dinar, upfront. Because I am on your side. And when you realise how many people are *not* on your side, everything is going to make sense. You see, there's only so much happiness in the world, and those who have it are keeping it from you. They are hoarding happiness, they are taking your share, and you have to fight back.'

'So how do you fight back?' The Blame Salesman's voice was quiet now, conspiratorial. 'How do you make the fake people suffer? I'll tell you how. Because the world works for them – because the world is rigged in their favour – you have to trash the world. Because they have everything, they have everything to lose. Because you have nothing, you have nothing to lose. That is the source of your power. You have to smash what they love, you have to squeeze the tears out of their faces. And those tears will be to you like the finest wine.'

The hall erupted. People cheered and pumped their fists, and the boy felt a surge of wellbeing. He was no longer the odd one out. Here were hundreds of people just like him, good people – the victims of a vast conspiracy. At the same time, they were superior people, because they knew who was to blame, who was grinding them into the mud.

The Blame Salesman went on for a long time, boasting of his prowess with women, of his independence and wealth, his contempt for the polite conventions that masked, he said, the Conspiracy of the Lie. By the time his orations ended, everyone in the hall was sweating with rage and vindication. They chanted and stamped their feet. They descended on the stalls where the Blame Salesman's attractive assistants were selling his books and pamphlets. They queued to meet the Blame Salesman himself in a brightly lit side-room where he shook their hands.

The boy trembled in that queue, awaiting his turn.

'What do I do,' he asked, 'about those people?'

'What people?' the Blame Salesman said, casting quick glances past the boy.

'The people who are taking my share of happiness.'

'It's like I said. Do things that will drive them crazy. Make them feel what it is to be you. Then you will come to feel what it's like to be them.'

The boy took this advice to heart. He set about planning ways to relieve his feelings of resentment.

The first opportunity came unexpectedly. A young group of friends was planning a day at the seaside. He was on the periphery of this group of very condescending people, but by making every effort to seem agreeable, he was able to get himself invited.

Now, one girl in that party was especially attractive and infuriating to the boy. She laughed too much with her shapely mouth and her gentleness was provoking. When they had arrived at the seaside, she suggested that they explore the rock-pool nearby. Everybody knew that the girl was interested in nature, and thanks to that interest, she was able to point out and identify all of the ugly creatures that inhabited the rock-pool. One of these, a large green crab, scuttled out of some seaweed with its pincers raised. The girl – and the others who wanted her to approve of them – gathered around the crab.

The boy found a large, smooth stone and brought it down, with all his strength, on the carapace of the crab. The crab's shell shattered and the stone bore down on the living softness beneath. It was, the boy felt, horrible and exhilarating, especially when he looked up to see the mouths of his so-called friends hanging open.

'What did you do that for?' the pretty girl cried, and there were tears already in her eyes.

The boy stood up straight with the rock in his fist. 'Why not?' he said. 'It's no use to anyone. You said yourself, it isn't even edible.'

The others gathered about the crab like mourners at a funeral. Nobody spoke to the boy for the rest of the day, and this persuaded him that he had been right to upset them, for their ethics were nothing but a performance to assert their moral superiority over real people like him.

A few weeks later, the boy moved out of his parents' house and began renting a room with some students. He had been reading the Blame Salesman's books and pamphlets, and consequently knew exactly how to seem pleasant and progressive to the smug young people who were looking for a roommate.

At first, the boy was cheerful and quiet, ready to do his bit to keep the shared house clean, washing his own and others' dishes. The fake people he was living with gave the impression of liking him, and this made him doubt his strategy. However, every one of them had a sweetheart, and whenever, late in the evening, the boy suggested that they play a game or go out for a drink, the others made up excuses not to go with him. He heard their sighs of pleasure and contentment and planned his revenge.

A few days later, the boy went looking for the Blame Salesman. He found him in a nearby city, and attended his rally, where the Blame Salesman gave the same speech as before. The boy stood, afterwards, in the long and sweating queue.

'I wrecked our house,' he said at last, when his turn came.

'Didn't it feel good?'

'I smashed everything.'

'And your housemates were scared, right? All that schooling and they didn't know what to do.'

'The girls cried.'

'Sweet female tears!'

'Our landlord kicked us out and now I have nowhere to live.'

'But do they, do *they*? Look kid,' the Blame Salesman said, but already he was glancing over the boy's shoulder at the lengthening queue. 'You stood up for yourself. You should be proud. Now if you follow my tough-looking associate, he'll arrange your payment.'

'Payment?'

'For my time. I hate to take it, but I have costs, right? Believe me, it's money well spent.'

The boy handed over all the money he had in his pocket. He felt confused, exhilarated by renewed contact with the Blame Salesman yet unsettled by unfamiliar emotions. He was having second thoughts, he doubted himself, and these were signs of weakness. The Blame Salesman warned against weakness. Showing signs of it was a terrible mistake. The boy gave himself a talking to in the Blame Salesman's voice. He was not going to be tamed so easily. The solution was to step up his guerrilla attacks on the nice and the good.

What could he do, what act of defiance against the Lie, could persuade the world that he was not to be trifled with?

The answer came in the form of a girl. She was plain compared to the beauties that paraded in his daydreams, and shy compared to the self-assured women he resented. She worked in a coffee shop, where he began to drink coffee every day. They fell to chatting, and because the boy was acting his nicest, sappiest self, the girl began to laugh at his jokes, she flicked the hair from her forehead and rested approving eyes on his face. It was exciting. The boy had a skip in his step. He looked forward to seeing the girl each morning, for with each passing day, she was more in his power, and he was not accustomed to feeling powerful. He took her out for walks in the park. They went to the theatre. They sat for hours beside the fountain in town, where gradually the girl opened up to him, telling him of her childhood, of her hopes and fears for the future. The boy had read his books and pamphlets. He knew that it was necessary to listen, or appear to listen, for many hours at a stretch to what a girl had to say. This, more than anything, was essential to imprisoning a person's heart. The tactic made sense to him. When had *he* ever been listened to? Who had ever cared – apart from his mother and father, and now this plain, smiling girl from a coffee shop – to hear what he had to say?

In time, the girl invited the boy to meet her parents. They would, she said, be delighted to know him.

He felt overcome with nerves, in the days and hours before the appointment. At last, the moment came when the girl's mother and father opened their front door to welcome in their daughter's new sweetheart.

The boy's knees shook beneath the table as they sat for dinner. The girl was smiling at him. Her mother and her father were also smiling, and he told himself that there was condescension in those smiles, that they were fake – they had to be, for these were fake people, only he was real. Even so, he had to drink several glasses of wine before he found the courage to complete his mission.

He picked up the plate that contained his dessert. He licked it like a famished bear. He burped noisily and wiped his mouth with the tablecloth. He found he could not meet anyone's gaze as he mounted the table and began to kick the other plates into the girl's lap and the laps of her astonished parents. Finally, drunkenly, the boy informed the girl that she was ugly and dull, and picking up the bottle of red wine, he emptied it over her head.

The girl fled to her room, her mother chasing after her. The boy descended sheepishly from the table and did not dare look at the girl's father, even as the man grabbed him by the collar and flung him this way and that, among the ruins of the evening meal, and slapped his face with the flat of his hand. The boy tried to sneer as the blows fell, but his face was wet with tears. He could hear the girl's howls and sobs upstairs as the father dragged him into the hallway, opened the front door and flung him powerfully into the night.

'All of that,' the father yelled, 'to humiliate an innocent. She loved you, you fool. She was sitting on that branch while you sawed it away, sniggering at the thought of her scream as she fell. And all the while, you were sitting on the same branch.'

The boy would remember little of the hours that followed his triumph. He awoke in the woods outside town, with a quaking head and a feeling of desolation. Despite his thirst, and his aching limbs, and the hornet's nest throbbing in his skull, he ran and ran, until he came to the nearby town where, only a few days ago, he had spoken to the Blame Salesman. But the hall was dark and empty. Gone were the glamorous assistants. Gone were the sullen security guards. Gone were the slogans, the balloons and banners and bookstalls. Gone, too, his chance, so briefly offered, so cheaply given away, at happiness.

What else did you expect? That's just the way things are in this world.

6
Pigs
Fred Pearce

Once upon a time there was an old mother pig. She had three little pigs and not enough food to feed them. So, when they were old enough, she sent them out into the world to seek their fortunes.

The first little pig was ambitious and went to the city to make money. He got a job in a factory and bought a brick house. It was a sturdy house and looked like it could withstand anything.

The second little pig cleared some land from the forest to grow crops to feed himself. He made his house out of sticks.

The third little pig went deep into the forest and built a home from straw that he found there. He hunted the forest animals and picked its fruits. His brothers said he was lazy not to get a job or till the land, but he said this was the best way to live.

Soon, the world began to change. The factory in the city shut, the climate changed and brought drought to the countryside. A wolf began to roam the land.

First, the wolf went to the city pig's house. He was hungry and thought the pig would make a good meal. He knocked on the door and said: 'Little pig. Little pig. Let me in. Let me in.'

The city pig saw the wolf's big paws through the keyhole, so he answered back: 'No. No. By the hairs on my chinny chin chin, I will not let you in.'

But the wolf replied: 'Your job has gone and you owe me money for your house. You must pay me or go. So I'll huff and I'll puff, and I'll blow your house down.'

So he huffed and he puffed. It was hard work, but the house had been badly built by the wolf's workers. So eventually he blew the house down – and took the bricks as payment for the debt.

But he did not get his meal. The city pig escaped. He ran away to hide with the second little pig at his country farm.

The wolf was still hungry, so he followed him. When the wolf came to the house made of sticks, he smelled the pigs inside, and his mouth began to water as he thought about the fine dinner they would make.

So he knocked on the door and said: 'Little pigs. Little pigs. Let me in. Let me in.'

But the little pigs saw the wolf's pointy ears through the door, so they answered back: 'No. No. By the hairs on our chinny chin chins, we will not let you in.'

So the wolf said: 'But I have a piece of paper from the government. I now own your land. So I'll huff and I'll puff and I'll blow your house down.'

It was hard work. But the sticks of the country pig's house were dry because it had not rained and it was hot. So the wolf huffed and puffed and blew the house down.

The wolf was still hungry, and he tried to catch both pigs to eat. But he was too greedy and the two little pigs scrambled away as fast as their little trotters would carry them. They ran into the forest, where they thought it would be safe. They eventually arrived at the straw house of the forest pig.

The wolf lost them in the chase. It was a long time since he had lived in the forest, and he did not know his way around any more. And he was very hungry, because he no longer knew which fruits he could eat.

But he sniffed the trail of the little pigs and eventually he found the house of straw. He could smell them inside. They would make a lovely feast, he thought.

So again, the wolf knocked on the door and said: 'Little pigs. Little pigs. Let me in. Let me in.'

The little pigs answered back: 'No. No. Not by the hairs on our chinny chin chins.' So the wolf showed his teeth and he said: 'I'll huff and I'll puff and I'll blow your house down.'

But the forest pig had done well. His brothers no longer called him lazy. They could see his house of straw was well-made. And they could see the wolf was thin and tired after his long journey chasing the two pigs through the forest.

They laughed, as he huffed and he puffed. And then huffed and huffed, and puffed and puffed some more. But the wolf could not blow the house down.

But he was even more hungry now. So he climbed on to the roof and jumped head first down the chimney.

The wolf landed at the feet of the pigs. He was dazed and nearly dead from his days in the forest and the bang on his head.

So the three pigs discussed what to do with him. The city pig said they should cut him into pieces and sell the meat for money. Maybe then he could buy new bricks and rebuild his house. The country pig said they should eat him themselves, because his crops had failed.

But the forest pigs said he had better food in the forest than a wolf. He said they should instead save the wolf and help him recover. This was the way of the forest. What you did not need, you did not waste. The more animals in the forest the better.

So the three pigs nursed the wolf. And a strange thing happened. Under their care, and fed on the fruits of the forest, the wolf's features slowly became less wolf-like. His paws and his ears and his teeth were less like a wolf, and he lost his love for pig meat.

And stranger still, the pigs became less piggy too.

Living in the forest, they were growing hair on their pink bodies. Like the wild boars that lived there. The wolf looked more like the pigs, and the pigs looked a bit more like the wolf. The house in the city and the farm in the fields were soon forgotten, and they all lived happily ever after.

7

Pintura, One Two Three

Deborah Rim Moiso

So' stato alla montagna alla Sibilla
Dove la neve non se strugge mai
Dove la neve non se strugge mai
E c'ho trovato la caval morella
Che non è doma e non se fa domare
Ma se je arrivo a mette' brije e sella
Le serenate jele fo' pagar

I went to the mountain, to the Sybil
Where snow never melts
Where snow never melts
And there I found the auburn mare
That is not tame and will not be tamed
But if I can harness and saddle her
I'll have her pay for every serenade

Pintura. One, two, three. I have tales to tell about this place. Tales for the telling – tales for troubled times. I have an inkling that this might help you, the reader, prepare somewhat for the storm ahead. We've had storms here before. This is the land of the earthquake of 2016, these are troubled lands.

Meet me in the heart of the Sybilline mountains—go ahead, fish out a map on your tablet or phone. This is the greenwood of the Apennines, mid-way down the dorsal backbone of Italy. The dragon's scales. An epoch of epochs of sea-life, sedimented deep, then rising up, in waves of rock and soil, that mount and froth and never crash down.

The mountains form a chain of folds and bends, immense, unknowable. Untamable.

Villages are built around water sources, or along a bridge, in the foothills. Above the villages are the forests. Then, 300 metres or so higher up, the high pastures begin. The greenest of green grass and alpine flowers. The flower gentian is our totem, the eagle our bird.

Life in these small towns has gone on for thousands of years, planting lentils and, later, potatoes, growing fruit and vegetables in small, sheltered gardens, leading the sheep and cattle up and down the mountains, according to season. In winter, humans and animals alike would retreat to the stone houses, huddled together to await the thaw. For half the year, anything higher than 1,000 metres above sea level was left untouched, left for the animals and the faeries. Every Spring, the wild and the tame worlds met again, their encounter celebrated by the ringing of a hundred bells from the livestock, from the church towers, strung around the back of the villagers' frame drums.

In this landscape, food cannot reliably grow higher up than 1,000 metres. For this reason, or perhaps because of old pacts, treaties and long-forgotten agreements with the mountain spirits, humans do not live in the peaks year-round. Buildings above 1,000 metres are essentially wrong, tolerated only as temporary shelter. There are few of them, of simple character. Oldest are the shepherds' huts, which look like miniature chapels, protected by kindly statues of Mother Mary, Our Lady of the Mountains immutable, pagan or Christian, wood or stone, mountain mama.

Later, as humanity reached levels of prosperity which allowed it to go exploring just for the heck of it, came mountain hikers' and climber's refuges, where the hearth stays lit. Warm places, large, full of bunk-beds, ruled by hospitality and open doors. You might notice that such lodges are subject to daily mishaps. A broken pipeline today, a landslide on the path tomorrow, just to keep cheeky humans in check, keep the rules clear: *you are NOT here to stay.*

And then there are the ski resorts, built much later, when all pacts and treaties and spirit-talk was long forgotten. Nowadays, people have the audacity of living up here, one-thousand-three-hundred metres above sea level. It has become quite easy to settle in the high peaks, now that the valley's supermarkets lie a quick car-ride away. One can see the sea, on clear days, over the landscaped fields of the Marques.

Pintura is one of these places. A tiny village of 13 houses, around an abandoned ski lift. Pintura, "the painting". A place built in the wrong place. And in the *completely* wrong era, as there is soon to be no-more-no-more-no-snow-no-more-snow-here. It's an unlikely place, each house a tale. I'll tell you three.

ONE
A fox lived in the restaurant kitchen

The first building you meet coming off the road is a large, squat, red, wooden restaurant. A flag blows in the wind in front of it, red white and green. The restaurant is closed all winter, and open all summer. Summer starts when the tourists come. The family who owns it lives far, near Macerata, along the coast. They came back last Spring to find the pantry plundered.

The pantry was plundered, in fact, by a fox, who lived under the big kitchen hearth. A slab of limestone and a hole dug beside it. If the stone is hot, the fire is lit—humans are home—stay put. If the stone is cold— time to sniff the air.

Carefully.

Smell of ashes and dust. Smell of old conversations and trail maps. Smell of melted snow, sometimes. Memories of smell of melted snow, more likely.

Old shoes.

Fox comes out, slowly slowly, ears alert. /\ /\

But, later, Fox settles in, finds comfort. Hangs out by the lean-to window. If a car approaches the main square, Fox looks out—that is the sensible thing to do, what you do, we all do, when you live in such a small, isolated place, you keep a look-out.

It's the farmer's jeep, come to switch the water pump on for the cows. Fox relaxes. Fox enjoys the wooden benches, picks out some cheese and ham to taste.

The valley's chicken coops are quiet and safe, this year.

Fox curls up in the upstairs bedroom, dreams of Spring.

TWO
Mushroom seasons

In front of the restaurant you'll notice a hotel—it's the largest building around.

Built with something more than 40 rooms: can you imagine the high hopes, high dreams? Was it ever full? Actually, yes, before the earthquake it would fill up each and every summer, for the lady who owns it, the formidable Linda, rented it out to the priests for their youth camps, and then it was full, full, full of feet and hands and sweaty armpits and hollers and shrugs and volleyballs and self-doubt and acne. And flip-flops. Plenty of flip-flops.

I've seen her toast to the success of yet another busy season with two priests at her table, toast with the bitter *digestif* we make with gentian root, stuffing wads of banknotes in her brasserie, laughing loud and emptying her shot glass in one go.

For the rest of the year, in the quiet seasons, when you would expect Linda to be living elsewhere, in places with shops, post offices and good internet reception, and maybe come up to Pintura, as people do, in the weekends, Linda lived in the hotel alone. She found no interest in the company of valley people. She watched television, kept a look-out on the village square, and did the things mountain people do. Picked raspberries, made jam. In autumn, it's all about the mushrooms.

All along the mountain fields in these parts, the green, green pastures are interspersed with vast circles of a deeper, darker hue. Sometimes they are so vertical, on the mountain face in front of you, you cannot imagine climbing up there yourself. The circles are fairy circles, that is, they are the outer ring of a web of mycelium growing in the first centimetres of the thin, black mountain soil. Fine threads of white fungi spread quietly under the surface, spread out, year by year, in rings like tree rings, and exude sugars to feed the grass, turning it a darker green. In Spring, all along the border of the circle sprout fat white mushrooms, which we pick, although it's forbidden, – park rules – but we do it anyhow.

Peace, you see, is apparent. Nature reserves in Italy are frontlines of environmental conflict. Continuous, low-intensity, and ongoing. There is no more real wilderness here, it is all an ancient web of pastoral use and reciprocal influence. The mountains are cultivated, tended, grafted, softly slowly bent to humanity's usage. Humanity too, does not go unchanged in this deal. And so, the park authorities juggle, or ignore, to their peril, the needs and entrenched privileges of hunters, farmers and shepherds, and the newer needs of hikers, trekkers and bikers. Criss-crossing paths of tension are everywhere, subtle. You can sometimes feel in your skin when you cross a boundary, a border. It's like being close to the field of the cow pastures' electric fences, when the hairs on your skin stand up.

In autumn, it's to the deeper forest Linda goes to hunt for mushrooms. *Porcini*, *boletus edulis*, brown capped and delicious. At dawn she heads out with her basket and stick, around midday she heads back, basket full. She eats some pasta, or bread and cheese, and takes a nap. In the afternoon, she prepares the mushrooms for preserving year-round. Some she slices finely and lays on racks to dry. Others she cuts in larger chunks, boils for a few minutes in water and vinegar, and puts in jars with olive oil and laurel leaves. You must always prepare the mushrooms you've picked yourself. This is a rule.

Sometimes she spoke to nobody for days. Other times, she might meet another mushroom hunter in the forest. Some would have a dog with them, for company, and for protection. Others were solitary, like herself. Some knew her name, from having stayed in the hotel in the past. Others did not. People are cordial, in these situations, and more often than not exchange truths about where treasures are to be found. The image of mushroom hunters always hiding their spots in utmost secrecy from one another, whilst completely true outside of the forest, loses its pull once under the trees. Linda and the other hunters point in various directions: this spot will be good this year, wait for the rain, the moon, a lot were found over in that valley last week by so-and-so, let's hope this weather holds, good year, good day, good day to you.

The first ten days of October went by in this fashion. And a few days more.

At the end of October 2016, the ground shook so hard, Linda decided to leave the mountains for the coast. She packed her basket in the car. On the 30 October, the hotel cracked open in two, like a nut.

The jars in the pantry smashed to the ground, olive oil all over the carpeting, pieces of mushrooms, chunks of cement.

But you know Linda. She drove back up to Pintura the next season, parked her car, barely glanced over at her broken hotel, hoisted her basket out of the car, and headed for the woods.

THREE
Time stopped, and therefore

The house I am staying in belongs to two sisters. It's the one painted green, to the left of the main square, with tall fences all around and a thick metal gate. When the sisters' young mother died, time stopped, and therefore.

Therefore, the sprinklers go on every summer day at 9 in the morning and again at 7 in the evening, despite the pastures all around being the greenest of greens.

Therefore, the gates are made of cement, but made to look like wooden branches, like a petrified forest of old.

Therefore, doors open and close, lights go on, all hours of the night. The sisters are light sleepers.

Therefore, the cakes and cookies served for breakfast come wrapped in thin, transparent plastic, like it's still 1986.

Therefore, these lamps. These heavy drapes. This furniture.

Therefore, dare I say it, there was no earthquake, in this house.

Time stopped, for good or bad. Nothing happens here. The sprinklers go on and off in the lawn and we are all safe.

Safe from the wild boars stomping outside the gates on summer nights. Safe from the call of the stag in heat down in the oak forest, bellowing below us. Safe from the ground swelling and shaking, the roofs smashing and falling, the walls crumbling and shattering and cracking, glass from the windows everywhere, furniture crashing to the ground and catching you underneath, your arms, your legs, your sleep interrupted so.

There are two spinster sisters here, and I believe they are under a spell. A spell to save them from their own wilderness. Which spell can't be a good thing, for sure, but hey, we did survive, didn't we, and we are here, to tell the story, which somebody must do, at some point, for the absence of the narrator is our worst nightmare, worst fear, worse than any trouble, earthquake, or change.

A spell, we were saying, to avoid them ending up like their mother, she who tumbled to her death down a cliff, while climbing up the mountain path to meet her lover at the Rifugio del Fargno, 1800 metres above sea level, perched up on the peak of an ancient stone wave, 500 metres above Pintura. Down the valley she fell, all the way to the Rio Sacro, the Sacred River, which feeds into the river Fiastrone, its cold waters flowing into the Fiastra reservoir, its green waters flowing out and down into the fertile valleys and into the Chienti and down to the Adriatic, sweet mountain water tumbling down to meet the sea.

Down the valley she fell, besides the Faeries' well, the Faeries' waterfall. There is a story here about that cleft in the mountains, farther along the mountain range. That is the path the Faeries made, as they ran back from the village festival, running fast, running hard, back to their Mistress and Queen, Sybil the teller of fortunes, back to her enchanted cave-kingdom under the mountains.

These are no twinkly, dragonfly-winged fairies with glittery dust in their curls. These are feral, hooved powers, with hares' ears and goats' feet, beautiful with laughter, horrid if viewed in

Just
The
Right
Light,
reflected from the icicles of the old glaciers. Not much left of those, melting drip by drip they are, melting, going, going, gone.

And they wanted to go down to the village, they did, to dance with the shepherds and the farmers, skipping and hopping to the sound of the fiddle, the accordion and the drum, beating the ground with their hooved feet (hidden under wide skirts, of course), one-foot two-feet, like children in a game, the hopscotch *saltarello*.

"Be back before the rooster crows" – she bellowed, their Queen.

In the same fashion, the sister's mother ran, skipped and hopped up to the Fargno, lovely beautiful starlit place that it is, a squat and stocky cement construction beloved by all those who walk and hike these lands. Nestled up high, where there are clouds forever and Mount Bove towering over it, like a placid giant about to hoist the building and all its inhabitants straight up to the Milky Way.

She ran, and she fell, and that was that.

There are flocks of black birds nesting in that mountain, mourning her fall. Their wings did not break it.

Up above, her lover waited.

Down below, her children wailed. Her husband woke, and cursed the flow of time.

That morning and forever, as the Fairies rushed into Sybil's cave, as the sun shone through the peaks in early morning, the Queen of that mountain, in her anger at their tardiness and, moreover, at their damned fascination with village life, commanded the roof of the cave to crumble, blocking the entrance forever.

E come sono belle queste fate
Però je crocchia i piè come alle capre
Però je crocchia i piè come alle capre
E vanno saltellando a mo' di lepre
E ballano in paese lo saltarello
La notte fino a'lo cantar del gallo.

How beautiful these Faeries are
But their feet crackle like goats'
But their feet crackle like goats'
And they jump along like hares.
And dance the *saltarello* in the village
At night until the rooster crows.

Author's note:
"Pintura, One Two Three" is a little suite of more or less true stories about the Apennine mountains. It deals with the relationship of humanity and nature in the high peaks. As glaciers melt and snowfall stops being a predictable occurrence, this is where I go walking, listening, and hunting for hope and meaning. It is set in the village of Pintura, a small

group of houses built in the 1970s around a ski resort. In the late summer of 2016, an earthquake turned most buildings into piles of rubble, harshly revealing the foolishness of dreams of development and "progress".

For human life in the peaks to go on, the stories now must take a different turn, delving into the deeper layer of connections woven by mushrooms, forest animals, birds and waterfalls, shepherds and foxes, stones and visions, songs and folk-tales. So that we may inhabit the mountains with understanding and love, recognising our place as a part in a much larger Story.

I picked these tales up while hiking in 2014 and in 2019 with Alessandro Porro and with Chiara Maiullari, and wish to thank my friends for their company in listening deep. The verses that open and close the tale are stornelli, the traditional songs of this land. These two I learnt from Roberto Leonardi – *grazie*!

8
Briar Rose and the Trees
Hamish Fyfe

'... and having been kissed, the Princess Briar Rose woke from her long sleep. The Prince and she were married and lived happily to the end of their days.' Or so it is said...

Kissing her suitor for the first time, blood from the finger she had cut one hundred years earlier suddenly flowed freely into the Prince's flaxen hair. Seeing this, and seeking to save him from any discomfort, Briar Rose went to wipe the blood away with the sleeve of her raiment. But the Prince held her wrist firmly and placed it by her side where it continued to bleed in tiny red drops. As they fell into the dusty ground, the drops of blood turned an angry purple, then dried quickly leaving no trace.

In the days before the wedding everyone wanted to see the Princess and she travelled the land meeting the rich and poor, the powerful and the weak. The people took the shy young woman to their hearts wherever she went. Even the Prince himself became more popular when he went with Briar Rose at his side. So loved was she that the people came to call her the Princess 'Aurora', the special light of the dawn. Every one of the gifts that the Princess had received from the wise women who had attended her birth were there for all to see. Beauty, intelligence, kindness, bravery, all the virtues that a person might want to bestow on a child were hers. The curse that had held her asleep for a hundred years in the Castle was surely broken now. No one seemed to think, not even the wisest people in the land, that these blessings might become a burden – the very treasure-burden that was to continue the curse of Briar Rose.

The night before the wedding, as the Prince was deciding on a suitable sword to wear the next day, he reached for the one that had so resolutely cut its way through the great bramble that had protected the Princess for a hundred years. Suddenly he remembered the words of the old man who had warned him not to go into the deadly briar tangle that made the Princess and her castle so impregnable. The great thorn hedge had claimed the lives of many young men whose bones still hung in the deepest parts of it.

'Don't go son. Once you get into that hedge no power on earth will get you out.'

Remembering the old man's words cast a shadow across his preparations for the wedding. Much to his shame he had begun to feel a little uneasy about the effortless perfection of his future wife and to wonder how, with his own limited virtue, he would be able to match such a paragon. The old man's warning not to go into the hedge rang in his ears as loudly as a church bell.

'How stupid I am,' thought the Prince suddenly. 'The Briar Rose is everything any man could want.

She is perfect. How could I harbour any doubts?' Thus the Prince prepared for his wedding enveloped in a shadow cast by his most secret thoughts.

The Great Wedding brought people from many neighbouring kingdoms and thousands made long journeys to be present even though they could not actually see the wedding take place. Royal Parks close to the Palace were opened up and the people danced, ate and even slept there. Their affection for the Princess seemed to grow and grow. The day of the wedding came quickly. Any doubts that the Prince might have had were banished as soon as he saw Briar Rose walk up the cathedral steps so bravely and so gracefully.

Looking on at all this from a safe distance and carefully disguised, the wise woman who had not been invited to welcome the Princess when she was newborn, and so had put a curse on the tiny baby, smiled a slow grin of satisfaction. 'My curse was not as simple as they thought,' she muttered to herself. 'My sisters have blessed the child with virtues alone. She will never be illogical, unreliable and self-centred, greedy, frightened or wrong. And so, she will never know real love, which is to be loved despite one's failings or even because of them. This truly is a curse and I will test the young lovers to see how their love survives this surfeit of goodness, and with that she left to lay her trap.

The wedding came and went with great splendour and the country gradually settled down again to its usual slow pace.

The Princess enjoyed the company of others but had found a beautiful natural arbour of trees, close to the Castle Wall, in which she could be alone when she needed to be. The trees that made the arbour had lived longer even than she had. Amongst the trees she felt that life was neither hard nor easy, the least distant rustle of leaves at the top of a tree was felt at the deepest roots but in their hearts they were always still.

One day, as the Prince stood quite still nearby, hoping to see his wife, the spiteful wise woman crept into the arbour and turned herself, in an instant, into a tiny grey moth. The moth flitted onto the Prince's shoulder where it began to whisper urgently to the Prince in dusty tones.

'I have noticed how much you love your wife Majesty, and the affection she has for you, but I am sure she would love you more if you expressed your love by building a marvellous new Summer House here on this spot that she is so fond of. What better material to make the building and its furnishings from than the trees your wife so adores?' These can easily be replaced and more saplings can be planted to make up for any loss,' said the tiny dusty grey moth.

Taking the moth's advice, and knowing the Princess would be away visiting her subjects in the countryside, the Prince took the opportunity to cut down the trees in the arbour to build the great summerhouse. 'What a wonderful surprise this is', thought the Prince, '... how pleased my wife will be.' Using only the finest wood to construct the summerhouse, the unwanted trees and bushes were discarded in a huge jumbled heap to be burned later. When it was done, the Prince was heard to say that it was indeed a good day's work and retired to await the return of his wife.

On her return the Princess was heartbroken. A great spoil of mangled and discarded wood and a shiny cold little palace was all that was left of her precious place. The Briar Rose could not be consoled and began, for the first time in her life, to feel angry.

Demanding that she be left alone she stared at the tangled wood pile – all that remained of the trees she had loved – and as she did so she became aware of a tiny dark hole at the very centre of the seemingly impenetrable pile of thorn, blackberry and oak. As she approached, she looked carefully at it, staring into its dark centre until her eyes began to sting. The longer she stared the more she knew that she must follow the darkness as it opened graciously and carefully to allow her in. Without hesitation she moved further and further into the envelope of broken and splintered wood.

Despite the scratches and cuts inflicted on her flesh, she pushed closer to the centre of the pile. As one branch moved, another moved as a result and the thorns dug deeper into her flesh. She knew now that what she did to the great jumble of wood she did to herself. Each part of the web was part of the whole. Suddenly the Briar Rose threw her head back and laughed. As she did so the sharpness of the thorns in her flesh drew blood from a hundred tiny cuts but she laughed all the more. People saw the scars from these cuts for the rest of her life.

Briar Rose could see now that she had indeed been cursed, not by the wise woman who had sentenced her to sleep for a hundred years, but by the others who had gifted her only light, beauty and virtue.

Not having seen the Princess for some time the Prince wondered if she might be in the new Summerhouse and made his way there to see her. Since he could not see her he called out, but received no reply. Calling again a little louder he still heard nothing and he was about to leave the remains of the glade when he heard a gentle voice that seemed to be coming from a tangle of dead wood. The tiny voice was calling to him. 'Your Majesty, the heart of another is a dark forest', it said. 'If you are truly to love the Princess Briar Rose you will follow her into the dark centre of the wood and bring the Princess back into whatever light you might find.'

The Prince had no knife or sword to cut through the thorny, twisted, pile and he was afraid. The words of the old man imploring him not to go into the dreadful hedge to rescue the Princess rang in his ears, but suddenly he heard the gentle voice of Briar Rose. At this the Prince advanced into the jumble of wood. On he went until he knew he was reaching its centre. He could not see, but he could feel the presence of the Princess. When they met they reached out in the dark and began gently to remove the thorns from each other, one at a time. When they had finished, and the thorns were gone, the woodpile vanished and they were left alone in the light of the garden, the special light of the dawn.

Watching this, the little moth that had alighted on the Prince's shoulder flew away angrily beating its wings as it went and was never seen again.

9

The Lokator

Andrew Simms

Unhappy, but not sure who to blame, the local people were distracted one day when a man in a multi-coloured coat appeared in the town square.

Three friends, Karel, Needah and Alice, lost in their own play on the steps of the Town Hall, were the only ones not immediately drawn to him.

Above them, staring blank-faced through the high windows of a building designed to impress, were a group of town councillors, known as the Elders, momentarily diverted from some piece of weighty council business, involving maps, charts and graphs.

There was no shortage of troublesome issues for them to discuss, including a forthcoming local election on which their positions depended.

Good jobs were hard to come by. Available work was either low paid, or otherwise unattractive to the longer established local population. But nature, and the local economy, it turned out, abhor a vacuum. Word spread and others from places with lower pay arrived to pick the fruit, pluck the salads and gather the vegetables from the market gardening that the area was famous for, grown in farms large and small around the town.

Over time, family members of the farm workers came too and filled other unattractive, jobs, doing the town's cleaning and poorly paid care work.

If they expected gratitude (they didn't, just to be allowed to live in peace) there was none. Quite the opposite. Tensions rose.

Karel, Needah and Alice knew little of it. Yet. They had a special bond born of experience, even though their backgrounds were diverse, and they and their bond will matter later in this story. Karel's parents worked on the farms, Needah's mother was a councillor, while Alice's family had lived in the same modest, terraced house for at least three generations. Karel could not walk and relied on a wheelchair, Needah could not hear and Alice was blind. This made them all different enough to be left out of the other children's play. Difference can always be difficult – but children are acutely aware of it. Yet what made them different also gave them something in common, enough to form an unbreakable ring of friendship.

Back in the crowded town square, Nigel Hamlyn was breaking into a well-worn but, he knew, effective speech. After flamboyantly removing his coloured cloak – a trademark of the election campaign, covered with equally colourful promises that were untroubled by facts – with a practised swirl, he revealed a smarter dressed operator. He had a sharp, flinty-eyed, ability to see what might incite an audience, which he used in speeches to carve into clear shape the vague feelings they had of being abandoned, or perhaps betrayed, by the modern world.

He didn't so much speak, as barked bonhomie, a barrage of words that slapped you on the back like a boisterous greeting in a bar. He understood you, would speak on your behalf, and be brave enough to name the darker fears and dislikes you thought, but dare not say.

Of these there were plenty, because stories in the local newspaper and on the radio station had been filling people's minds with worries for weeks. And, all the stories implied that these fears had a certain kind of face, one that was relatively new to the area.

'Plants pulled-up in new ornamental gardens', 'Graffiti dishonours war memorial', 'Widow robbed of week's pension on doorstep', 'Jobs and homes going to newcomers complains councillor' – a drip, splash, drip of discontent filled the news pages and phone-in programmes.

In truth these were things that had been reported forever. The difference now was how the stories were told. The gardens were a place 'known to be popular with the children of the farm workers'. Conversely, the war memorial was not so popular with the town's newer arrivals, 'few of whom attended its memorial ceremonies.' In anonymous comments from neighbours who lived on the widow's street, it was reported that 'we don't know, but we see faces that aren't from round here.'

The councillor in question was soon to switch allegiance from the Blue Party to Nigel Hamlyn's electoral caravan, the Location Party (strapline: 'We are where you are'). Hamlyn himself adopted 'the Lokator' as a nickname because of his ability to tell where people were at. The odd spelling was merely an affectation borrowed from the entertainment industry that seemed to go down well on social media.

From their window high in the Town Hall, the Elders gazed with flickers of approval from their meeting – about which no minutes were being taken – at what was happening down below.

In turn, the crowd listening to Nigel looked-on with something closer to contempt at those they assumed to be from the farm worker's community, but who were also, remember, cleaners and cooks and carers. Some just then were nervously skirting the square to do their weekend shopping. They were people who seemed different in a few ways, different clothes, different accents, and whatever some looked like on arrival in the town, working in the fields for months had given them a distinctive weathered appearance.

Over time words crept into the stories of local disturbances, and the way they wove the newer arrivals into them. Words like 'swarm', 'tide', 'overwhelmed' and, even, 'invasion' and, most extreme of all, 'infestation'.

To keep their control of the town in the forthcoming election, the elite needed to be seen to act, but at the same time they wanted – how to put it? – To keep their hands clean. After all, they considered themselves civilised people.

Their answer was to invite Nigel Hamlyn to town. He would clear the problem away, clean the streets, for a price. It would be a large donation to a private campaign account, and key posts in the council for any successful Location Party candidates in the election.

Hamlyn had a track record and a trick. He would arrive in a troubled community where a minority could be blamed for its problems and play a tune that applied pressure from two sides, until the minority felt pressured to leave. His bark brought vigilantes onto the streets until windows were broken, children felt intimidated on their way to school, names were called and fights broke out. But, he also pretended a kind of sympathy for the targeted groups, said he had friends among them and liked the 'law abiding' ones. A secret weapon was an employment agency he touted to them, which offered work in call and distribution centres, where the zero hours contracts appeared to offer hourly pay that was better than whatever was available locally. No one ever checked if this was true. A range of rumours, some very dark indeed, circulated too about Hamlyn outside of the mainstream media, against which he held a number of legal restraints, preventing publication.

The combination of a hostile atmosphere and an apparent way out was effective. Soon people began to disappear from the town. But other problems then emerged.

Cafes and restaurants complained of staff shortages. Offices and the local hospital could not find enough cleaners. Agencies and retirement homes ran out of care workers. Finally, and perhaps the biggest problem, there were not enough willing hands left to pick, pluck and pull the fruit, salad and vegetables in the farms and market gardens that were the source of much of the town's wealth.

Yet the elders seemed unconcerned. Stories of vandalised monuments and muggings had been replaced in the local paper and radio station chatter with upbeat tales of wonderful new economic potential. As the election approached, they said, here was a chance for rebirth.

But the Elders made a mistake. They thought they could control Hamlyn, and that they could get away without paying him. They also had secrets, some of which would not remain secret. One of which might explain why they seemed blasé about the dying of the farm trade formerly relied on by the town.

When Hamlyn discovered that he, the great trickster, had been tricked, his flinty eyes sharpened, seeking the revenge he was about to take. He was angry, but a certain glee curled up the corners of his mouth, because for him, who had no real material worries in the world and was never touched by the consequences of the strife he stirred, this was fundamentally a game, how he made life interesting and felt good about himself. The vengeance he'd take would be perfect: he would use all his skills, contacts and knowledge, and the result would leave them guessing for generations, perhaps forever.

Just then, though, the Elders were feeling extremely pleased with themselves. The focus of local dissatisfaction had been removed, and done so in a way that gave them plausible deniability for peddling division. They had 'outsourced' the solution.

They were pleased too because of one of their secrets, and because they thought they'd been very clever.

Those maps, charts and graphs were again spread across the Elder's board table, the wood polished so brightly that it reflected their smiles of self-satisfaction. More than just marking the area around the town with its farms, orchards and market gardens, it unrolled the Elder's vision for the future, if vision is the right word.

Three years before, secret studies revealed that beneath the roots of the fruit trees and vegetables was another crop, much less nutritious but potentially far more profitable. Even better from their perspective, it could be harvested without the need for migrant labour and, indeed, fewer workers all told.

Huge deposits of gas had been found, ready for fracking. In the Elder's calculation the town would grow rich, and they, themselves, would grow richer than most. Quietly they had been buying farmland, something which would not have seemed unusual, as most were landowners already.

Contamination of the groundwater from the fracking could be handled, they estimated, for the town's water supply, but it would mean a one-way ticket for the area away from growing its own food. A price worth paying they thought. And the Lokator? They'd done him a favour by giving him another platform, and he'd done them a favour by clearing people off the land and making the struggling farmers feel they had little option but to sell-up.

The Elders smiled inwardly at all the local media stories which had so effectively prepared the ground. Reporters on local papers and radio stations are horribly overworked and rely on tip-offs, something the Elders were happy, usually anonymously, to supply. But the truth, of course, was never quite how it was reported.

For example, the Elder who passed on the story about plants pulled up in the new ornamental gardens was able to do so because it was him who pulled them out. And the reason the gardens were popular with the children of farm workers was, in fact, because they were part of community gardening scheme which helped maintain some of the plant beds. A similar explanation lay behind the graffiti on the war memorial, and the reason few from the migrant community had attended ceremonies, well, their representatives had not been invited. An oversight...

The story of the widow – an aunt of one of the Elders – was a little different. Her pension money had in fact been taken by her great nephew, the Elder's son, an opportunistic theft on one of his visits to buy alcohol for his friends. She lied to the reporter to cover her family's blushes. And, the faces seen on her street that 'weren't from round here', they were also the community gardening group who cleared and planted some of the overgrown verges and even helped some of the more infirm pensioners on the street tend their gardens. The letter from the councillor about jobs and homes going to newcomers simply contained no facts that could be checked to justify the claim. Drip, splash, drip. The problem to which the Lokator, apparently, was the solution had been spun into existence. But who would ever connect the dots?

Where the Elders' judgement failed them, however, was in underestimating the venom of a vain and thwarted man.

The Elders woke on election morning, brimming with confidence, not only assured that they had solved the town's self-created problems, but also that they were about to do very well for themselves. Yet, sitting at their breakfast tables, mentally planning their victorious walks around town, they all felt as if something was missing.

It didn't feel like success. It was too... quiet. Where was the normal rattle of homes readying themselves for the day, of children crashing in and out of bathrooms, and up and down stairs? Come to that where, in fact, were the children? Increasingly urgent parental calls went unanswered. A great and nauseating silence fell in house after house. But in at least one home on each street, an unearthly scream of realisation sounded from a parent distraught with fear. Something terrible, inexplicable, had happened. All the town's children were gone.

If you are hoping for some kind of explanation about what happened to them; a resolution – however awful – you will be disappointed. Their fates were never discovered. There were, of course, many theories and rumours, some more lurid and some more likely than others. A peculiar plague or a chemical release hushed up by the authorities. Some kind of mass hypnotism meant the children were there but could not be seen. A generation so outraged by its parents appalling behaviour and ruining of the world they were to inherit, that they simply decided to rise up and leave. Some even suggested it was the work of a modern day Pied Piper.

All that we truly know, we know because one of the things that you have been told isn't quite, completely, true. Not all the children disappeared. Three remained: Karel, Needah and Alice.

Whatever befell the other children, somehow left these three friends untouched. And it was being different that accidentally saved them. How much did they know? Not a lot. But the night before, many encrypted messages buzzed between the town's children – something exciting was happening somewhere, but to find out what it was, and where it was, you had to be at a certain place, at a certain time. As the route that took the sounds of life from the town, the road rumoured to have harboured this rendezvous point was later renamed Silent Avenue.

Karel, Needah and Alice were vaguely aware that something was happening, and that is all they could say, but had – as usual – been lost in their own play. And, besides, even in daytime let alone at night, the town was not wheelchair friendly, Needah heard no activity in the street and Alice had no use for the social media Apps used by others their age. They communicated and did things differently, in a way that allowed for one who could not walk, one who could not hear, and one who could not see. They only did what they all could do. They were also very used to '*not*' doing what all the other children did.

So Karel, Needah and Alice did not disappear. If anything, they 'reappeared'. Ignored by most for much of their lives they now became, in fact, very important. They were the only children left, and seeing them, from their different backgrounds – one the child of migrants, one of a councillor and one of a long-established, worker's family – allowed the townspeople to see the possibility of different groups thriving together. In its shock the town looked to them, as magical in their survival as the other's disappearance seemed – it was whispered – almost demonic. It made the three children virtually untouchable.

This meant that when the Elders' plan to frack the former farms for gas became known, Karel, Needah and Alice protested. Every time a test well for gas was dug they were there, putting their bodies across the access roads. Public opinion swung away from the

Elders. People missed the sense of identity that being a provider, one of the nation's great gardens, had given them. They didn't like the emptiness and the fact that so many other services no longer worked well either, or how the communal gardens, now untended, had become ragged and overgrown.

Increasingly frantic at how their plans were unravelling the Elders gathered again at the Town Hall to look for a way to cast themselves as both victims, like everyone else, and also potential saviours of the town. They could endure most of their losses, but they could not imagine losing their power.

Then on a television screen in the boardroom which carried a news channel and was always on, the faces of Karel, Needah and Alice appeared. It was live and the town's three remaining, untouchable children were being interviewed within sight of the boardroom window in the Town Square.

Needah's mother rushed to turn on the television's sound. What they heard froze the Elders' where they stood, and they could feel the children's words prizing their fingers from the grip of control that they had held over the town for as long as anyone could remember. Karel, Needah and Alice were not trying to take control for themselves, they were announcing a randomly selected assembly of local people to debate and decide on the town's future.

It would be a Citizen's Assembly to consider big questions about how the town would, for example, now welcome people from elsewhere, and about whether they would prefer to grow food or mine for gas. Local people gathered around them were smiling. The reporter was sympathetic and interested. The children's proposal seemed as untouchable as they were.

Author's note:
In medieval Europe in what is now northern Germany there were characters known as 'Lokators', who operated like recruiting agents. Upheavals and conflict left some regions depopulated, and the Lokators were hired by employers who needed workers. The original versions of the story of the Pied Piper made no mention of a town infested with rats, but were thought to stem from a real event in which a community – traditionally Hameln – lost its young people, possibly to disease or other tragedy, or maybe due to some kind of relocation. This period may have been full of perils, but there were no modern borders or passports restricting movement.

10

The Red Shoes

Anthea Lawson

"... there is a simple door waiting for us to walk through. On the other side are new feet. Go there. Crawl there if need be."

Clarissa Pinkola Estés

Nina stared at the flames, enjoying the difference between her slowly toasting front and the cool evening air at her back. She was still getting used to the feeling of food in her stomach after four days without, the press of bodies side to side round the fire after her time alone.

The grandmother leading this group of girls was still talking, but Nina didn't feel any urge to attend closely. It felt good to drop down into herself, to allow herself to relax. The older woman's voice was part of the smooth flow of sensation through her: the heat and light of the fire, the silhouette of trees on the ridge against the draining light, the glow inside from a difficult task completed. Her initiation was nearly over, and soon she would be counted as a woman.

"This one is very old, and has been used to say different things in the past," the grandmother was saying. Nina tuned in. This one had been telling good stories all week, before the girls went into the woods on their solo vigils, and especially since they got back. "Once upon a time, a long time and perhaps only a few days ago, there is a girl who is very poor. She has a big heart and great creative talents, which she uses to make her life as beautiful as she can. She can't afford proper shoes, and manages to patch together a beautiful pair out of scraps of red fabric. One day, as she walks to market, thinking about her dead mother, a golden carriage rolls up.

"A smartly dressed old woman looks out and offers the girl a comfortable life, if she wants it: she just has to step in. It looks a lot easier than the life she has. The girl climbs into the carriage.

"When they arrive at the old woman's house," the grandmother continued, "she is given fine new clothes, and told that they will go to buy proper shoes. The red homemade ones must be burned. At the shoemaker's the next day, the girl spies the most fabulous red shoes she has never even imagined. The old woman insists they choose something plainer, but her sight is poor. With the connivance of the shoemaker, who gives the girl a leery wink, they sneak the red shoes past the old woman, who pays for them without realising which ones they were. The first time the girl wears these shoes to church, the villagers point and stare, and soon her new guardian realises what has happened. She finds her a plain pair of clogs, and forbids the girl to wear the red shoes again."

The girls were all listening now, back from their reveries. Nina's friend Tani put another log on the fire and the nine of them edged closer. "The next Sunday, the girl can't help herself: she buckles on the red shoes. Leaning by the church door, red jacket falling open over a dirty white t-shirt, louche grin, is a soldier. He offers to polish the shoes with a rag, and she holds out each foot, enjoying the attention. He taps the soles with his stick and whispers, 'remember to stay for the dance.'

She thinks about that during the service, and also about the smell of this man, and when she emerges from the church, conscious of the many glances at her feet and the old woman's rage, there he is, looking for her. 'What beautiful dancing shoes,' he says. And that is it: she is dancing. Round the churchyard, down the lane.

"At first it is fun, but soon she wants to stop. And she can't. Eventually they corner her by the lychgate, hold her down and wrench the shoes off her feet. She's wild eyed, breathless, scared... but not scared enough to heed the old woman's furious warning, as she slams the shoes onto a high shelf. A few days later the shoes are still winking at the girl, and she takes them down and puts them on. Now, they make her dance faster, her body can barely keep up with her feet, she's whirling through the village, everyone staring horrified, into the graveyard where a spirit perched high in a yew tells her that she'll always keep dancing.

"Down the hill she goes, trying to pull the shoes

off. Nobody can help her, she dances for days, in and out of delirium. She's at her end, exhausted. As she dances past the executioner's house at the end of the village, she calls out for help. She asks him to cut her feet off, which he does. The shoes, her bloody feet still fused in them, dance away from the axe, down the road and over the horizon."

The grandmother stopped and looked into the flames. Nina felt Tani's knee shifting against her own but she couldn't look at her. None of them wanted to look up first. They couldn't risk eye contact when they hadn't yet worked out how to compose their faces. They sat like that while the sounds of the nonhuman world filled their silence: the new log shifting down into the fire bed, creatures rustling leaves, the faint cold rush of the stream below them. "Would anyone like to say anything?" asked the grandmother.

Tani spoke first. "Why are so many of the old stories full of such horrible things? I'm now stuck with this awful picture of the poor girl with bleeding legs and no feet. I don't want that in my head, thanks very much."

"What do you think is going on here?" asked the grandmother gently. These sixteen-year-olds had been through the initiation that everyone now experienced at their age, but they still had a lot to learn. Weeks away from their families and school, with a group of older women for the girls, older men for the boys. It led to a four day fast out on a hill on their own, no tent, no food, just the dawning of their own relationship with what was left of the nonhuman world after the times of violence, a sense of their own place in it, their own responsibilities towards it.

These initiation rites weren't the only thing that was done differently since the Great Shift, but the consensus was that they'd had the biggest effect on the health of people's minds, as well as their willingness to keep to the new food and travel limitations. When the changes first began, harvests were failing in the heat and people were panicking terribly. They'd tried sumptuary laws with strict punishments, since it was so obvious that leaving people to make their own choices hadn't worked before. But draconian prohibition on its own didn't work either, it never had.

Growing numbers of parents were already getting together to have their teenagers initiated into nature-respecting ways, and finally the lobbying of the increasingly influential coalition of ecopsychologists, nature lovers, and the geniuses who persuaded the entire cabinet to attend a *psilocybin* ceremony together, paid off.

The school calendar was rearranged, a network of wise men and women were trained. The indigenous peoples from other parts of the world who'd never stopped initiating their young, were offered a place at the heart of many programmes, which some of them were willing to take.

"What's going on here? I'll tell you, this is another of the stories from the time when men wrote the stories, so horrible things have to happen to girls,"

Tani grumbled. "We've done all this at school: there used to endless TV programmes and films and porn where young women get raped and murdered. I thought we'd developed past that now."

"Yes, that's true, those stopped a couple of generations ago. But this isn't quite the same. It's a much older story than his time, but it was collected and written down by a man during the time of violence, and he put his spin on it. For him it was another of those stories that warn girls to be nicely behaved or else."

"Bit late for her to learn to behave now she hasn't got any feet," muttered Tani.

"But do you know why we tell it now, my love?" The grandmother had become a patient woman, and this happened in almost every group she led. Tani scuffed at the embers with the heel of her boot.

"This one is like lots of these stories in which horrible things seem to happen to girls. It's really about instinct. The girl allows her instinct to become injured. She likes the look of an easy comfortable life, even though she's managing well on her wits, stitching her handmade shoes. The comfort of that gilded carriage looks like a chance to take it easy for a bit. But that's the decision that blunts her instinct, cuts her off from her true nature. Now she's easy prey for the new red shoes, and she starts making poor decisions – even as it becomes clear that they're trouble. She's drawn back to them again and again." The grandmother looked round. Several of the girls were nodding, pleased to have caught up. "You know the rest, now, don't you?"

"And that was us, our culture," says Nina.

"Exactly," says the grandmother. "We were captured, our instincts were captured, so we were easy prey for denial, for bad decisions. What were we captured by? Does anyone know?"

"Thinking we could kill the soil and insects and birds with chemicals in order to grow food cheaply?"

"... .thinking we can live without the rest of life on earth?"

"... that weird growth thing they used to have, where the money had to keep on getting bigger?"

"... that it was ok to steal land from other people?" The girls were all interrupting each other.

"Right," continued the grandmother. This group had learnt their history well. It went in better these days, now that teaching from kindergarten onwards included stories about what had gone wrong, about the stories that themselves had not helped. "And when we're captured, we yearn for what we've not got, our connection to our real soul. We thought we were separate from other nonhuman beings for such a long time, hundreds of years, probably thousands. So we were starved of our real connection, to everything else that lives and exists.

"The girl's obsession with the red shoes. We had lots of obsessions, like thinking that money always has to grow. In the story, her fixation on the shoes is what keeps the girl from her core instinct, which would otherwise tell her: something is wrong here. Until the Great Shift, our grandparents and their ancestors were blinded by those shoes. People who get taken by the red shoes think that whatever they're addicted to is going to save them. We thought that if we invented more technology, grew more money – which we could only do by killing nature – we'd be ok."

The grandmother paused, thinking about what had happened in her maternal grandparents' town when the food prices started spiking. "Cutting the shoes off is brutally painful but by then it's her only option. She's lost so much of the instinct that could have protected her against bad decisions earlier. It hurts to cut away from being addicted to destruction. But not having a foot to stand on: that's the point we reached. There wasn't enough food, fighting was spreading," she said.

"To cut that old culture's feet off, it wasn't easy but they had to do it. They had to hack off all those old ideas. To start again. Remember, she doesn't die in that story, she just has to start again... with a lot less than she had before.

"And that's why we tell this story to girls who are coming into their adult responsibilities. At regular points in our lifetimes, starting with what you've done these last few weeks, we leave our regular lives, our jobs trying to make the cities liveable again, to spend time in the green that is left, with the creatures that are left. To remember our instincts. To remember that we're not 'in' nature, we *are* nature. And it is all of our jobs to protect it.

"Come on, let's sleep. We're packing up camp in the morning."

11
Songbird and the Bwlch
Chris Nichols

I was born just after the separations.

Maybe you remember stories of that time, of when the council put patrols on the boundary in the Marches? It's an ancient border, they say. That makes sense; I have seen glimpses of an earth wall behind the towers. I've heard the wall is fearsome in some places, machine guarded, with searching lights.

But it's not that way here. This is a gateway province: *bwlch*, in our tongue. For me this wall has been my lifetime companion, a place of foraging and sometimes of rewards, and once a place of meeting. Yes, once a place of sacred meeting.

But that was long ago. They call me an elder now: I must be old, in bone at least. Forty-seven droughts, that is my age. Preserved for wisdom by my empty bed and empty belly, the villagers say. The mothers do wane first, that is certainly the way it is. Wise or not, I have something to say before the oak tree calls me back to its roots. I want to tell you what I've learned. No harm can come of it now. The council might curse my bones, but those will soon enough be dust, so let them curse if they will.

I will write this down in your tongue. Not so many this side speak this way now. After the separations most of the lisping soft speakers took themselves east, or their ways died with them here. We speak the tongue of the welshing-march, west of the separation. It suits us, this tongue, it follows the shape of the high hills and the dry winds. It fits our songs. They say you can hear the scorching sun in our poems.

How do I speak your tongue? The words were passed to me by mother, and to her by hers. My grandfather's grandfather was one of the last speakers in these parts they told me. A strange breed, a walker he was called, in the days when people passed either side of this wall at their own bidding. He came from a settlement in the eastern wild, Hay-in-the-Wire I heard it was called, a long-gone no-place. No one walks that way now, through those barren hills to reach what? Sometimes I heard stories from the convoy, when the guards came to me for comfort. They spoke of lawless horrors before the inner-wall. Why would you stress your flesh to watch nightmares spring from the dust?

But here I am, leading you into a wasteland of my own weaving; this isn't the story I want to tell you at all. I want to tell you about a songbird in a summer long ago. Thirty years almost, before we had felt the full heat of the sun. My parents carted luscious grapes from our hillside, deep red fruits so sweet the memory makes me smile. We carried them to the bwlch and beyond, to meet the convoy to the mainway. There was good trade in those days and the bwlch was open. Our fruits were cherished beyond the inner wall.

The mainway is still there, of course, but it's not guarded as it was. In those days there were rich cargoes to protect from the outlanders. That's what the council calls us freefolk. The separations addled peoples' minds, that's for sure, turning some into worker drones, some into hunters and turning everyone against someone. Perhaps that what walls do. They look like they protect something, but it's not so simple.

The heat years came, and our vineyard turned to dust. But our goats are hale. We swale the hillsides to catch the rain if it comes. There's food enough for those that know how to live here. But in the days before the sun-scorch had taken so many of the young, then I took our red grapes to the bwlch, and then was when I saw her.

She was with the guards, staying at the patrol post. But she wasn't one of them. She was a different kind. I saw her down in the hollows, looking closely at the flowering plants there. She didn't look at the plants the way I do. But still, I'd never seen anyone from the guard post use the hollow for anything more than a latrine. She was not like them.

She wasn't fearful when I first spoke. Curious, maybe. After all, the council didn't expect freefolk to speak their tongue, or to offer anything beyond trade. She showed me her device for capturing likenesses – I don't remember what she called it, though I've never seen the like before or since. It made the tiny patterns inside a foxglove leap out larger than life, as if you were seeing with a magic eye. She said her work was studying plants – inside the walls there are places where this happens, she said, even though the plants are all outside.

It was her that told me what it is like inside the walls. Before the separations, she said, there had been killing: fighting that no-one could heal. Men decided to do what men do, and had built walls. The boundary on the Marches was only one, and not the biggest. The inner-wall is magnificent she told me, and inside it is the capital where the council sits. Many people live inside the wall, in cities where you can travel for hours and days without leaving them behind. These cities are where she worked, studying plants. It is never dark there she told me. Busy as a hive, day and night. It sounded like a place of wonders, of its own kind. I felt sad that people there never could see the stars.

Some people do see the stars, she said, and trees and the ocean. If you are allowed, you can travel to the funlands. This is where the mainway goes now, taking people from inside the wall to beauty, in green hills in the south west, and northern lands if there is peace with the investors there. Some people travel to the very edges where water laps the rock. I have heard stories of these places, but I didn't know they were real.

She goes there sometimes, she told me: she had been there to plant gardens by the sea. The funlands are prized, held safe by the investors, and only a few of the investors folks allowed passage. Some people live there, the wardens and the hosts. Some of them practice the old crafts my grandmother used to speak off, making and baking and offering their work at markets in the ancient way. She told me the investors are kind, making sure these ways live on, to show visitors to the funlands.

I took her deeper into the hollow to show her the herbs I needed to heal my leg. We know our healing. We have herbs that can cure a weeping wound, and others for a griping belly. She was very interested in everything growing there, making impressions of it all in her magic eye lens, showing me each one and then hiding the likenesses away like a squirrel preparing for winter.

Inside the wall she said, my leg would be healed in a horsepetal. I told her that this plant wasn't one I knew, asking if she had a likeness to show me. She laughed, in a lovely way, that reminded me of a stream I knew as a child. She told me a horsepetal isn't a flower, it's a place where they do healing inside the walls.

She described one. It sounded scrubbed and full of lit bright rooms of remedies. It sounded fierce and awful to me: I couldn't imagine how any healing happened there. She said this is how they keep the investor's people alive for a hundred years. I think they measure ages differently. No one lives for a hundred years, that's not how people are.

We spent that afternoon together, walking far from the gateway, along the hollow seeking out every kind of plant I knew to show her. And when we reached the water place, she watched me make a poultice, a soft mossy pad crunched tight to draw out the healing heart of the plants. She washed my leg. Her touch was so soft. I tell you I remember it to this day. I didn't know someone could touch you as gently as that. It was so different to the hands of the convoy men. We walked back as the stars began to appear in the night, and once along the way she thought she heard a bird sing and we stopped heartbeat to heartbeat, hoping it would sing once more.

The next day she was gone, off to the funlands with the lapping water, to plant her gardens I expect. I felt her going like I felt the fading away of a beautiful song. It was easy to forget that she wasn't a freelander like me, that she was owned by the investors. She was so delightful, so soft. I wish I could have known her more.

Her going left a gap in me that I hadn't known before, so I have my own bwlch to guard. Sometimes it is a hungry place, longing her to come back and fill it full of softness. Other times it is something warm and full, like a bush in berry when the season has been kind. I think that's the place my wisdom comes from, if wisdom it is. In her coming, and in her going, I saw something I had never known. That the roots of the flowers feed from both sides of the wall, and that sometimes a songbird flies high above these borders, untouched by guardposts and searching lights.

Some of us are more like roots or more like songbirds; we are creatures unbound by walls. And for me there is a truth in that, a truth that warms me every time I think of her, like a song barely remembered, that I hum when the nights howl with the heat.

12
Foxhole
Emily Spiers

The room was cold and Geraldine shivered. Blank, shiny walls reflected the chill back at her, along with an indistinct image of her own form. Whatever drugs they had given her were certainly not benign this time. Her reflection wobbled as her sight blurred.

She curled in on herself, rolling herself up into as tight a ball as possible. She felt diseased. Smelled bad, a worrying scent she tried to ignore.

The machine started up its clicking and whirring again in the corner. Geraldine was familiar with machines that were larger than this one. Smellier ones whose noise she would usually run from. This one purred its way over to her and proceeded to arrange her in an upright position again. Twig-like metallic probes extending through the bars to pierce skin, pinch, tweak. Unable to scream due to the bindings around her nose and mouth, Geraldine endured.

Noah was sipping weak tea while he watched the monitor. The chill had seeped into his bones despite his insulated parka and he shivered. A thought passed through his mind that the chill was not only an external one. He was watching Subject 109 on the monitor as the GP-bot took her post-trial measurements. Ricky, the unit's chef, had dubbed her

Geraldine, after a previous girlfriend with the same sandy mane. He watched Geraldine twist as far as she could away from the robotic arms carrying out various tests simultaneously.

Noah worked at a privately funded lab somewhere in the steppes of central Asia. It was interminably tedious work. Geraldine was one of a litter of corsac foxes, a breed identified as prime carriers for LMX3.29z, which had been sent to the unit for testing.

After Douma, 20 years before, the Chemical Weapons Convention had seemed to weaken and crumble and by now it was open season for private chemical contractors like the one Noah worked for. Also being tested, although not in the same way as 109, he thought, was the GP-bot that was currently assessing her – bloods, resistance, mutation, virility of the strand over time.

GP-bot was theirs because of the potential risk to human testers of contamination. But he knew they were being rolled out in North America and the UK in what used to be local health centres. GP-bot. Capable of penetrating the shame and ignorance of even the most inarticulate of patients to get to the heart of the cancerous tumour, the STD, or bout of depression via sensors rather than language. Noah had long suspected that language was in fact the barrier to rather than the conduit of understanding. GP-bot seemed to prove his point.

Noah could see but not hear Ricky through the reinforced window to his lab. His gaze moved between

Ricky's slender frame, stooped over the stove in the kitchen, and Geraldine – Subject 109 – on the monitor screen.

[ACCESS GRANTED]
[RUN SCRIPT]
[EXECUTE]

'Oh Ricky, you're so fine, you're so fine, you blow my mind, hey Ricky!' Clap. Clap Clap.

Yes, I was singing. You remember that song? I wasn't sure if anyone could hear me, but I didn't really care at that point. At that time of the late afternoon... clap, clap, clap... the staff could fuck off unless they wanted their dinner served directly into their laps. Then I served, cleaned up, smoked a fag. The usual. I was in bed by 11.

Fuck, I hate this shitting place. These people. But, to be fair, as an ex-con, being the cook in a dodgy place like this was always as good as I was ever going to get. Noah is all right, I suppose. Then there was Geraldine. Poor fucker. The worst thing about this place isn't the male lab technicians – condescending scientists and other idiot geniuses somewhere on the spectrum.

The worst thing's the animals. The foxes, in particular. I'm sure Noah told you I took a shine to Geraldine because she reminded me of an ex-girlfriend of mine. Beautiful hair. She had something of the endurance runner about her.

I know you think I did it. I know Noah thinks that too. Look, I don't even know who you are. Never seen you until you turned up this morning in that chopper. Who are you?

Well you can all fuck off. Show me the evidence or suck my dick.

[SCRIPT EXECUTED]
[OVERRIDE COMPLETE]
[PROGRAMME COMPLETE]
[OUTHUMAN active]

By midnight on the night of Noah's first trial with Geraldine, she was gone. So were the other corsac foxes. Surveillance cameras, door and room sensors, AI units, all had seemed to cease functioning at 11.30 pm. The majority of the staff had been asleep, or passed out drunk in bed. There was nothing much else to do in winter. Noah's head hurt. She was gone. And with her LMX3.29z. They'd sent trackers out first thing in the morning but a fresh fall of snow had obliterated the trail.

He walked towards the interrogation room where they were still holding Ricky.

That clicking, whirring sound again. The twigs are back. Geraldine lifts her snout. The machine purrs at her. She sees its eyes for the first time. Scents fresh snow on its tracks. She grunts. Lifts her head higher, pulling herself up from the cage floor. She steps out of the open door.

13
View from the Train
Nicky Saunter

The first time she saw the fox it was trotting parallel to the train along a faintly worn path between two clumps of woodland. It was sleek and purposeful – a clearly defined russet fox shape against the grey-green of the tussocky grass.

It moved easily and efficiently through the landscape like a shark through the shallows. Its head was steady like a dancer and its tail flowed out behind, ending in a delicate dot of white paintbrush fur. For a fleeting moment she sensed its freedom and place in the pattern of things. It made her feel as if she could almost sense the sun's breath on her back, hear the wind whisk round her ears, smell the earthy grass under her feet.

A tree flashed past, close to the window and momentarily she lost sight of the fox. She sat forward in her seat, craning her neck, searching, as the countryside sped past. But the fox had gone. Down a hole or something – there was no way it could have reached the woodland in the few seconds it was out of view. She felt her heart racing and her face flush. A wave of nauseous claustrophobia swept down her body and she sat back, breathing deeply and concentrating on not being sick.

"Are you alright?" The man next to her had shifted in his seat, a look of concern on his rather handsome face.

"Sorry," she said, automatically, "I sometimes get this. I just need to take a few breaths."

He was smartly dressed with a neatly trimmed beard, a crisp white shirt and gold cufflinks. "I saw a fox." she blurted out, feeling ridiculous as the man nodded, turning back to his paper.

The train was slowing on its approach to the city and people began to move about, putting on coats, reaching bags down from the overhead luggage racks. She realised she was holding her breath and let the warm air out, misting up the cold glass and turning the scene outside into a blurry watercolor. The last mile of her daily commute slid by, mostly warehouses, back gardens and wasteland corners that were surprisingly wild, covered with buddleia and alive with butterflies.

At the station, the ticket barriers were broken again and the queue shuffled slowly along the platform, through the tunnel and into the square outside. It was a relief to be able to lengthen her stride as she took the quieter riverside path towards her office. There was a meeting at nine and she just had time to prepare, work out what to say in response to the strategic plan. The fox faded slowly from her mind like a disturbing dream – something unreal but important nonetheless.

She worked late and it was dark before she set out on the long trek home, stopping in the office washroom on her way out. Washing her hands, she noticed how the harsh overhead lighting brought out the red highlights in her hair. It looked good and she decided to colour it that evening.

A friend had given her a box of henna powder last birthday and she spent the evening applying the powdery herb mix, strolling about with a plastic bag pegged to her head until the dye took, and then shampooing out the grit for what seemed like hours. The results were worth the wait. She brushed out her thick hair and then tied it into a ponytail, enjoying the shock of the unfamiliar bright conker colour each time she swung past the hall mirror.

The second time she saw the fox, it saw her. As the train approached the same low lying field, trimmed with spiky, pollarded willow, she spotted it at once, this time slightly further into the field. The same long, slender back and poised head, this time standing and looking directly at the train. In his mouth he held a small rabbit, limp and soft, still warm, she imagined, from the kill. She felt a pang of sorrow and also a quickening of her heart, a rush of excitement and anticipation.

The fox looked up at her and lowered his head, placing the rabbit gently in front of his feet, nudging it once with his nose. Her mouth felt dry and she could taste the tang of metal.

"Are you alright?" This time it was a woman in the seat next to her. She was leaning in close and gesturing toward the magazine on the fold-down table before her. There were several large red drops of liquid quivering on the shiny surface of the glossy paper. "Have you got a nosebleed?"

"Oh thank you". She took the tissue offered by the woman, and put her hand to her nose, but it came away dry. She tasted tang again and realised the blood was coming from her mouth. Dabbing at it gently, she mumbled something about biting her tongue and the woman smiled sympathetically, before telling a rambling anecdote about her daughter biting her tongue at her own wedding and ruining her dress. But later on, when she examined her mouth in the mirror she found nothing wrong: no sign of injury on her tongue, no wobbly tooth, no bleeding gums.

On the way home, her eye was caught by a new shop next to the newsagent. It was a butcher's shop, tiled in blue and white, with shiny metal trays holding soft portions of glistening red and pink meats in all shapes and sizes. Slices, slabs, legs, breasts, haunches, wings, necks, loins and shanks. She rarely ate red meat but her mouth was watering, so she went in and bought a steak – a small one but good quality sirloin – for a treat.

Standing by the battered stove, she grilled it lightly in her favourite pan, bringing just a hint of brown to the outside before removing it from the heat. She had intended to serve it with new potatoes and salad, but could not be bothered and instead ate it on its own using just her fingers, tearing off bite-sized chunks and feeling the raw, uncooked flesh slip down her throat, warm and tender.

She slept well, windows open to the night air, listening to the neighbourhood dogs bark, owls hoot and cats yowl and scrap, and woke early when it was still dark. She could see the shapes of the furniture in her room quite clearly despite her blackout blinds. This was annoying, because she had thought the room quite dark enough before.

She could not bear the glare of streetlights and had designed the blinds specifically to block them out completely. But she could see quite clearly, so there must be light coming in from somewhere. She would find out where and fix it in the morning. There was also a strong smell in her room – musty, pungent – but not entirely unpleasant. Half asleep, she wondered if something had died and been trapped under the floorboards – a rat maybe? She made lists in her mind of how to tackle this problem; take up the boards, scour the room, clean the house from top to bottom. But when she woke again later with the alarm, the smell had disappeared along with her plans.

The last time she saw the fox, it was waiting for her. Her morning had started badly. Leaving the house, she had startled next door's cat, sunning on the adjoining wall. As she strode down the path towards the gate, the ginger tom, which normally greeted her with a flick of its tail, winding around her ankles, had fled before her in terror into the road and straight under a passing car.

She had no idea why and felt bad for the driver, a young man who looked like he had only just passed his test. Together they delivered the limp body to the next door neighbour, an elderly man who took it and retreated inside. It was so quick and shocking, and yet she felt surprisingly untouched by something that would previously have left her quite traumatised. She wondered at this new detachment – was her job making her uncaring perhaps? Should she speak to someone about it or would that make things worse?

She was still pondering this question as the train swayed towards the long straight section of fields and the distinctive gap between the woodlands. Even from a distance she could see the outline splash of colour against the green and knew it was her fox. Of course it wasn't her fox; just a wild animal in a field on her way to work.

To feel any further connection was plain silly; she was not a hippy and did not believe in reincarnation, so there could be no possible link between her and some random fox. Yet as the train drew level with it, she felt a wave of panic and knew she had to keep it in sight this time. She struggled up from her seat, pushing past the young woman in headphones beside her, and ran back down the carriage toward the vestibule, falling over luggage in the aisle, careening from side to side and leaving a trail of people tutting at her rudeness.

The door slid shut behind her and there was no one else in the lobby. It was louder out here, with the shake and rattle of the train unmuffled by the soft furnishings of the carriage interior. She ran to the small window pane in the door, and pressed her face onto its cold, hard surface. The fox was right there on the grassy field edge, facing the moving train, his golden eyes fixed on hers as the train moved past.

She felt a wave of relief and then one of fear, as his eyes left hers and he turned away as if he had forgotten something. He broke into a trot and headed in the direction of the wood, hesitating only once to stop and look back over his shoulder; a gaze of intense hunger that spoke directly and with such clarity that she knew what to do. Or her body seemed to know – because it flung open the door and leapt from the train.

She hit the ground hard but stayed on her feet, finding a new balance and strength in her haunches to absorb the drop and enough spring to take the first leap across the field. She could smell the grass close to her nostrils, damp from the dew and earthy; she could feel a breeze ruffling the hair on her back, bringing wafts of hay, hedge and hens like signal flags on a faraway ship.

She could no longer see or hear the train. She was fully alive and could feel the throbbing of blood through her veins. She felt her ears flick round toward her mate, now several paces in front and almost at the wood's edge.

Before he disappeared completely, she gathered her newfound strength and leapt towards him, bounding across the last stretch of grass – a flash of russet red fur melting into the dark of the tangled trees and the beckoning undergrowth.

14
Fairy Dust
Nick Robins

Midas was rich beyond measure, but knew he would never be able to touch his wealth.

He had conjured it out of nothingness, creating artificial quintillions that flattered his off-planet accounts. 'Fairy dust' his wealth manager on the spinning settlement of Vidar had called it, lips moist at the thought of the thin slices of fees she could earn for storing this extraordinary hoard that would never glimmer or glint.

From the beginning, Midas had a plan. First, he drip fed small trillions of his stash into those quaint bazaars that still traded dollar and yuan, creating a velocity of chaos that cheered his steampunk heart. He chuckled as he thought how he had become the saviour of that ancient thing called cash, as the peoples of Earth ripped their money out of their e-wallets and kept it snug in their pockets, their cushions and under their hats.

Next, he went after the cryptos. He had always spurned their company and hated to be described as one of their ilk. How could anyone think that these currencies were disruptive. How shockingly reactionary to even use the word coin when creating that thing formerly known as bitcoin. How foolishly physical it had been to rely on actual energy in so mundane a process as mining.

Midas revelled in the part he had played in their downfall in that searing September. The 'new Soros' chanted the news outlets. This was not just patronising, but fundamentally misinformed, mused Midas. Back on 16 September 1992, Soros had played with the once great British pound sterling, ushered in Black Wednesday and made a billion on the side. Speculation pure and simple.

Thirty years later, on 16 September 2022, Midas delivered a quick one-two with far deeper purpose. First he raided the cryptos, sucked them dry, closed them down, and sparked a salutary crash. Then he used the proceeds to buy all the world's firms still selling that dirty stuff called fossil fuels and closed them down too. 'Green Friday' they called it later.

And with the quadrillions he had left over, he took a tiny fragment and sprinkled it across the cities of smoke far below, turning power stations into spectacular parks, car parks into fun fairs, and motorways into palaces for the poor.

But Midas was bored. He was the richest man in all history. He had done what no-one had ever done before – actually implement a plan to the letter. He had freed the world of financial tyranny and ended the curse of climate change.

He wanted more, something to hold.

'Pass me my golden crown', he ordered.

The wonderful, butter-yellow circlet had first been worn by Croesus all those years ago. Midas was now far, far wealthier than anything Croesus could have dreamed of in Sardis.

He felt the cold of the metal for less than a second before the gleam ended in a shower of dust.

He lunged for his goblet of wine. That too dissolved into a slow dribble of dust.

He spun around and glared at the Earth through his space-station's window.

As he began to hammer on its window, he reflected with a smirk in that tiny millisecond that remained of his life, how quickly he had passed from being the all-powerful King of Fairy Dust to being just another piece of stardust.

There was nothing golden about it at all.

15
The Partnership
Ed Mayo

"Why?"

"We sold two beds last month, Jonno," said the store manager, "and I just can't keep you on. I am sorry mate, but just two beds a month and by the winter sales, I'll be bankrupt."

"Come on, you owe me. I thought we were partners," said Jonno.

"As if! You take no responsibility. I open up, I close up. You're on the till but I am the boss and it is my business. But listen, I am sorry, Jonno. You know as well as I do, we just don't get the footfall we need anymore here in the shopping centre. I am going to keep going, as I reckon people still have to sleep, but I just can't afford to employ you. I can't afford to employ anyone."

Jonno glanced at the store manager, who shrugged, reached down and handed over a brown A4 envelope marked in capitals 'JONNO KIDD – FINAL PAY AND P60'.

As he did so a passer by passed by and, catching Jonno's eye, stepped into the shop. Wearing an olive green scarf over a double-breasted indigo coat, she seemed out of place, more sophisticated than the shopping centre regulars. She stepped lightly around the beds towards them. As she came close, Jonno drew breath and smiled.

"Samantha, wow. What are you doing back here? I thought you had gone for good."

"I'm Sam now, Jonno. And I am back from Brussels. I'm starting a new business and I thought where better? Redditch, West Midlands! So I'm home. Or I'm not, I'm looking to buy. I will be. Now, can you talk? I want to know everything that has happened."

Together, they stepped down the broad spiral staircase leading down to the ground floor and as they walked, Jonno pulled up the zip on his ill-fitting, worn sweatshirt and lifted his tracksuit bottoms to give air to his pride and joy, his Puma trainers.

Entering the café, Sam clicked her fingers for the waitress. After they had both ordered, they sat down to catch up on the ten years since they were classmates at the Crabbs Cross Academy. A lot had happened... the recession years after Brexit, the trade deal with America, the football title for Aston Villa, with all its Chinese money, and relegation for West Bromwich Albion.

"Marie and I got married in 2020. She's a teaching assistant. No kids, it's the dogs for me. And I'm still in the same block," explained Jonno. "My older sister, you'll remember, she's in one of the new Redditch Housing Co-op units, all Norwegian. She is the elected residents chair. The new development down Robert Owen Way, the eco-houses – you'll remember the trash and the piss going home down that lane after school. Well, the clean up is all down to her and her friends."

"With me, to be honest, it is not easy. I have been unlucky. I'm in debt to my eyeballs, no job, as of half an hour ago. It is not my fault, of course. It's the economy. I just need a break. But, what about you?"

"Life has been good, genuinely good since I left," said Sam, pushing back her teacup. "But I'm coming home, mainly because I do feel as if I belong here. But also, I do want to put something back.

"So, work was great. I won't bore you with it, but I have done pretty well for myself – fashion work, consultancy. After so long away, though, I really wanted to come home. Out there, it got be as if every new conversation started with a question mark; as if I was a second class European. I have been on my own, too, for the last few years. Don't get me started on Italian men. So, here's the plan, here's the pitch... "

"In the nineteenth century, nine out of every ten needles in the world were made here, in Redditch," declared Sam, her eyes wide, her hands chopping the table in a mimicry of past manufacturing. "The world of fashion owes a debt to the West Midlands.

"Well, needles are not the point now, but with all this weather madness, solar power is, and fashion certainly hasn't gone away. So... I've been working. I've done the designs, got the patents for, drumroll... window blinds with a difference. Here's how it works. On every slat, we put a strip of solar PV. Cool Blinds, I call it: 'keep cool, keep the planet cool'.

"So, I've been looking around for an old warehouse nearby I can turn into a small assembly and I have found one just – outside of town. I have got pre-orders, I have got bank credit. Why don't you join in, help me out, Jonno? I am going to need it."

"Samantha... Sam, you know what school was like. I've got no skills. I can't sell beds, so I can't sell blinds. I wouldn't know fashion or street cred if a paving stone hit me on the head. And I haven't got the fingers or the patience to be putting things on slats."

"OK, here is what could work," replied Sam after a pause, drawing closer across the table. "What I need is a gate keeper, a reliable person to open the gates in the morning when the blinds come in by truck, and open the gates in the afternoon when the finished goods go out."

"I dunno, Sam."

"All you have to do is to push the button. The gate goes up. You push the button, the gate goes down. Twice a day."

"I'd feel odd you being my boss."

"OK, well," she drew breath. This is what she was home for, she thought. "We will be partners. Straight down the middle. It will take time to build, but we can share profits 50/50. Like one of your sister's co-ops."

They shook hands. Jonno went home to explain his new career move to his partner, Marie. Sitting round their wood veneer kitchen table, he was over the moon. He had cash from the bedding shop and a new job in a new business. She wanted to know more about Sam.

Next week, Jonno started at the Cool Blinds factory. He had a cabin to work in, with a kettle, fridge and radio. In the morning, he pressed the button. The gate went up and the lorry came in with the goods for assembly. At the end of the afternoon, he pressed the button. The lorry went out with the assembled goods for distribution.

His sister wished him luck and sent him a curious link on social media, quoting someone called George Jacob Holyoake about partnerships. He had been born nearby, but in the nineteenth century when the town ruled the world of needles and fishhooks. The quote was "only fools don't learn and since you cannot make co-operators out of fools, it is prudent to ensure that they do not overrun the co-operative."

Jonno did his job and the business went well – spectacularly so.

At the end of every month, Sam and Jonno sat down to look at the sales list and divide between them, 50/50, the money they had earned. She counted out the notes and passed Jonno his share, tucked into a white A4 envelope.

After six months, it won awards for Sam and Jonno at the Redditch Chambers of Commerce Dinner – 'Cool Blinds a Local Business Success'. After nine months, it was featured in the Birmingham Post – 'Local Business Proves a Cool Winner'. After eighteen months of trading, with Sam working all hours and using every connection she had, Idris Elba ordered blinds for his holiday home in Britain. The firm was picked up in the fashion pages of the *Daily Telegraph* – 'The Return of Cool Britannia'.

After six months, Jonno felt his swagger coming back. The income was good, the credit cards paid off. After nine months, he and Marie moved into a semi-detached house overlooking the local park. After eighteen months, Jonno started to feel disquiet. Was it all really fair?

Life is not fair – that was his Dad's favourite saying. His sister probably disagreed, but Jonno knew different. All his life, people had taken advantage of him, he thought. His Dad was right. It is obvious that life is not a team sport; it is about standing up for yourself.

The trouble with the country, and here, Jonno was in daily agreement with the headlines of the daily newspaper he read, is that people are taking advantage of us – cheats, immigrants, Europeans, whingers. We are not getting what we deserve.

As he sat during the day in his cabin, with his newspaper and his mug of tea, the hits of his 1990s Good Times radio station playing loud, waiting on the lorry to fill up, waiting for it to look to him to press the button for the gate to rise, his sense of frustration grew.

Late one morning, Sam drove up in her metallic blue electric sports car. As Jonno pressed his button for the gate to go up, she pressed her button to wind down the car window and waved at him, laughing as she drove in.

Late one night, talking to Marie in bed, he rehearsed a speech he was going to give Sam the next morning. She had been out travelling a lot. Seeing journalists, she said. Winning orders for exports, she said. Commissioning prototypes for solar blinds for electric cars, she said.

Who really was the boss? Two years since their conversation in the shopping centre café, it was time to talk. It was Jonno's turn, he felt, to do the talking.

They met in the café again. Like others huddled over their tea or cappuccino, they were both drying off from the storm outside. Jonno said what was on his mind:

"The whole set up, Cool Blinds, it is not fair. Look, we are supposed to be partners, we are supposed to share things fifty / fifty. But why? Is that right... ?

"Look, it is me who presses the button... me who lets the lorry in, with all the parts. It is me who presses the button when the lorry is ready to leave, with all the blinds. I press the button. I should be getting more than fifty per cent. I should be the boss."

The next day, the partnership dissolved.

16
Outnumbered
Geoff Mead

DO YOU WANT TO LIVE FOREVER?
Apply to Signor Leonardo Bonacci
Piazza del Duomo, Pisa

I saw the poster pinned to a tree near our warren a long time ago, when I was too young to know better. I showed it to my best friend Coniglio and he agreed that it looked too good to ignore. So, we hopped onto a passing carriage and went into town to meet Signor Bonacci. We soon found him loitering outside the cathedral.

"We've come about the poster," I said. My companion thumped the ground to lend his support. He's never been much of a talker.

"Excellent," said Signor Bonacci. "What are your names?"

"I'm Coniglia," I said, "and this is Coniglio. You can call me Connie. We definitely want to live forever. What's involved?"

"Well," he replied. "I'm a mathematician and I need a couple of bright bunnies like you, to prove my latest theory. Do you know anything about arithmetic?"

"We rabbits are pretty good at multiplication," I said.

"Multiplication skills are essential for this experiment," he said.

"Experiment?" I queried. "Nothing dangerous, I hope?"

"No. No," he replied. "It's all in my book *Liber Abaci*. It's a new method for creating a sublimely beautiful sequence of numbers, whose proportions approximate ever more closely to the so-called Golden Ratio. Or to put it more mathematically, $F_n = F_{n-1} + F_{n-2}$"

"Means nothing to me," I said. "What do we actually have to do?"

"Wait exactly one month, then produce two offspring, one male and one female. In another month, you produce two more and so do your offspring. Next month, the same thing and so on. Can you do that, without fail?"

"Shouldn't be a problem," I said. "We're notoriously prolific."

"Good," he said. "It's also essential that you all live forever. It won't work otherwise."

"And how do you suggest we do that?"

"My friend Constantine the Alchemist has created an elixir that will make you and your descendants immortal." Signor Bonacci produced a small glass phial from under his robes. "Three drops will do it."

"Why don't you take it yourself?" I asked.

"Apparently, it only works for rabbits," he said.

I waggled my ears. "Lucky for us, eh?"

"The only other thing," concluded Signor Bonacci, "is to make sure you count the total number of rabbits each month."

"And this will prove your theory, will it?" I asked.

"I'm sure it will," he replied. "Do we have a deal?"

"We'll give it a go," I confirmed. "Should be a piece of cake."

Things started well enough. By the end of the first year there were 376 of us gambolling in the field. In another six months the total had gone up to a cosy 6,764. As the second year drew to a close, I made it 121,392. Soon our numbers were increasing so fast it was almost impossible to keep up. But a deal is a deal and we kept on going.

We began in 1202. That's 817 years or 9,804 months ago and there's an awful lot of us now. Would you like to know how many? Signor Bonacci told us the formula for that too: $\sum_{(n)} = F_{(n+2)} - 1$. It's pretty easy to calculate with a computer. The answer is a 1,029-digit number:

59474068521395332358208041 9138
47775812328929696959608504036014
48059415628820794044091 9768378
70981 92761 41655862926646019243
25358610864012336541 2103295484
9421011 354899118507295510 75046
87522820665816946416 5663368797
45846470755511 6834535701263439
112415331928220242890248384887
891755143409256276847950573299
44006586129388817491 6740531064
59453694075896180252979598 2850
293585641 81261 6792186458891802

025191271001123069122828878800
249783096978738975877175782909
700167630501643299792868225808
346229551988053696625350503319
617152150134804722010257661044
723121976697418200998111301302
046358853901615494158354191122
749185918714743096636861556951
018080177094132406103250248014
018241807326860628604699352374
211583858376356105877069324292
543661493663884828910892606831
554114593768625137125611464900
488133651899588899008364339026
235232815471792456374423585950
516297724326278691302787005164
925055599415607471149743217229
267765695175759096128012304092
890766108811984055905485486547
671140839745283147717548186143
550820671230398836771691251836
541220624895854757951824756592
570627194286028917498772359504
837167620309399299812320818418
915720043492502072292063545209
304552425151868871896882545666
750472284231574426180433034577
074234008078330221727616203270
037503213504842946475965532151
891683532934838201648537176881

8911073450694704016301660190830513250580753489143985777261656184127075934840622473674565476893725647612872116287260192710881230594261903554933138039093449875679504729858304446269430760455102286079722895888463747045471062889410708050723503160407141979950984378025334030000954496211537332023442129999879564469431680491800767938046117547485911333198923859309909473061805852498072529908877759703500828036134714330990040564592098041091042645626154583829315874986884545639106149519558338538008205574957995975434639933968116572234444572490432452103429135036807915190444363430861477758837229448533861811313620077876718535969628513918475222834172774556154516899458062863225333986711266549124577277596846161741360841419516433962459760415325277544277115144923113401473O5

Let me put that into perspective for you. The total number of stars in the universe is estimated to be about 1,000,000,000,000,000,000,000,000 (that's one billion trillion, a mere 22-digit number) which is approximately the same as the number of H_2O molecules in 10 drops of water. It turns out Signor Bonacci was right. There are now more rabbits than there are H_2O molecules in the Pacific Ocean. There is no name for a number that large.

We have evolved into the most intelligent (and indeed the only remaining) species on Earth. Unfortunately, in a couple more months the combined mass of rabbits will cause the planet to collapse into a black hole large enough to swallow the rest of the cosmos.

I rather wish I'd never seen that poster.

17
The Sleeping Giant of Lomah
Katie Kedward

The citizens of Lomah could not remember how the Wall around their city came to be there. In fact, the citizens of Lomah could not remember much about anything at all. The mucky smog that had smothered the city's skies for centuries, like grey icing on a grey cake, made their minds dull and indifferent. The Wall, which let no-one in and no-one out, had always towered above them and always would. That was that.

Lomah was immensely wealthy, and its people did very well for themselves. In accordance with the Liturgy of their High Priests, its citizens observed the nine-to-five diligently, heeded their consumption targets, and acknowledged personal responsibility for their eventual fate. It was the sort of place where everybody minded their own business, thank you very much.

And so when a girl called Sophie felt something small and hard drop onto her head one day, she was at first somewhat irritated. Things were not supposed to drop out of nowhere and interrupt a perfectly timed morning commute. But as she picked up the offending item, Sophie realised that it was not a pebble, as she had imagined. It was an exquisitely formed, russet-coloured seed.

She peered at it closely, dumbfounded, sensing something unfamiliar shift deep within her. What if... ? It would be heresy. And, worse, the neighbours would not consider it respectable behaviour at all. But curiosity resurrected a long-dead cat. She had to see – could it work? *Could it really be?*

Rushing home on sleepy Sigma-6 street after work, Sophie dragged her father to a dusty patch of earth in the alleyway behind their apartment block, and showed him the seed. "Where on earth did you find it?!" He whispered, caught like his daughter between unease and possibility. Yet as he held the little seed, something came back to him. He showed his daughter how to dig into the hard soil and plant the precious seed.

"Do you remember the last tree?" Sophie asked her father, as together they watered the patch. He didn't answer for a while, his face screwed up in concentration and mind operating like a rusty bicycle gear. "They told us it was weedy and sick – the last tree." He replied slowly. "A waste of space, a parasite, undeserving of Lomah's support... worthless."

"But I do remember learning about the Forests – in schoolbooks, before they... . Oh, the stories were magnificent!" He cried, telling her of how some trees grew as tall as skyscrapers, how their vast structures housed myriad life forms, and how each one was part of an even greater and even more magnificent whole still. He recounted a dimly-remembered old story of vast forests blanketing the unknown fells beyond the wall, holding the forces of nature in delicate harmony.

Suddenly Sophie gasped. A bright green shoot had emerged out of the barren earth and was visibly growing taller with each word her father spoke. As they both fell silent and bent down to examine the tiny sprout, it too paused its progress, and quivered in the still, evening air. "It looks like it grows from words?" Sophie's father suggested.

"Not any old words," his daughter said. "Stories – it was growing from your story." She leapt up. "We must put the call out for more. We must help it!"

And so it was that the residents of Sigma-6 Street awoke the next morning to find an unusual flyer on their doorsteps, and car windscreens.

> SEEKING FABLES, TALES, SAGAS, SERIALS, AND YARNS – LONG OR SHORT. MEMORIES AND DREAMS WELCOME. GATHER AT THE ALLEY BEHIND BLOCK J. DAILY FROM 5:01PM.

Most of the street's residents considered this highly irregular. Conversation with neighbours was generally confined to brief comments on the weather, the traffic, or the merits of the latest car model, as their dogs sniffed each other. But some on Sigma-6 Street had never been asked to tell a story before, people whose words had been long ignored by the city of Lomah.

The first visitors to the Tree that evening, therefore, were not well-to-do literary or creative types, but a motley group of eccentrics, lonely pensioners, and other social misfits. They were fascinated by the hungry green sprout. Gathering around it, one by one they tentatively offered their untold dreams and experiences – and so began the first stories of a new beginning.

Stammering Stan told everyone how he had smuggled snake eggs out of the zoo in his underpants in order to start his reptile collection; Mavis the Cat Lady recounted her steamy affair with a famous newsreader a few decades back; and Old Ma Laurel spoke of a recent dream in which she had been standing on the shoulders of all her ancestors – only to have fallen off by the time she realised.

By the end of the evening, the skinny tree-shoot had grown a little taller and a little sturdier. The group left feeling also somewhat more robust in stature – their minds clearer, their ears sharper.

Each evening the stories continued, and the audience grew alongside the little sapling. Friends brought friends who brought friends. People shared food, ale, and teapots filled with peppermint tea. And together, nestled in that forgotten, neighbourhood nether-zone, they consumed stories of every flavour. They laughed at the whimsical, contested the controversial, and shed silent tears at the sorrowful.

Above them, the sapling's delicate fronds grew taller, fuller; and the clouds above began, imperceptibly, to clear.

Soon enough it became impossible to hide, that for the first time in living memory, Lomah once again had a growing, thriving Tree. People came to Sigma-6 Street from all corners of the city to touch the swirling gnarls of its bark and marvel at its strange beauty.

Many saw it at first as a sort of tourist attraction: an opportunity to try out the new camera; something different to distract one's pestering offspring; a destination to take a date to that was (rarely for Lomah) free of charge. But, after a few hours of breathing the clean air under the canopy, each day-tripper left with sparks flying unseen in their heads, and a handful of stories to share around the dinner table.

Trees were technically illegal, according to Section 7.3 of the Liturgy; but the High Priests turned a blind and unconcerned eye. "Let them have their curiosity," the Chief Priest drawled to his council, as he skimmed through the tabloid's double spread ("TREE-MANIA AT SIGMA-6!"), "I fail to see why we should be worried about a single prehistoric weed."

Here, the council made two mistakes they would later come to regret. The first, a result of below-average horticultural knowledge, was that one weed can, in fact, become very pervasive indeed. Deep, deep downwards and outwards, the Tree's roots were growing an unseen network beyond Sigma-6 Street and across the city. The second mistake was failing to notice the stories and the impact they had.

The tree remained in the alleyway behind Block J, but like its sprawling roots, a newly fired imagination went rampant – and strange things began to happen in Lomah. Seeds were salvaged from 3D-printed vegetables, and neighbourhood gardens sprang up on street corners; heretical (but hilarious) artwork sabotaged billboards and street ads; whacky ideas ricocheted around recurrent street parties like infinite pinballs.

People began to see what had, in fact, always been there: the absence of the High Priests from much of their daily lives; the many unfortunate souls residing in the city's cracks; the absurdity of the Liturgy. And above all, the mystery of the Wall: its grey conformity, its monstrous waste-pumping pipes ("where does it all go?"), and its vast, bleak finality.

They saw, they wondered, and a conversation began.

One day, for the first time in months, the Chief Priest looked out of the window at the rest of the city and realised that he could see the Tree. Despite it being many miles away from the High Temple, he could see that it had grown to a great height, almost as tall as the temple's tallest spire. He studied its broad twisted trunk, its majestic canopy, each knotted branch, and each kinked twig. Then he looked down at the streets below and watched his subjects with growing panic.

He no longer saw individuals marooned on tiny islands of indifference. He saw an enormous magical blanket covering the city, its threads connecting peoples and places and ideas and dreams in a chaotic tangled web. It was engulfing rules and boundaries and structures, it was shifting and shimmering in a dynamic dance, and it was push-push-pushing against that final frontier: the Wall. The Chief Priest downed the rest of his cold coffee, and called the council.

When the people of Lomah saw the matte-black helicopter drones rise from the High Temple and head towards Sigma-6 Street, they knew exactly what was happening – deep down they had always known. The alarm was raised, rippling through the web faster than any drone can fly, and citizens spilled onto the street in their droves, racing towards the Tree as fast as they could go. Above them the drones bellowed the official message:

"THE TREE HAS BEEN IDENTIFIED AS A THREAT TO THE PROSPERITY OF LOMAH. IT WILL BE TERMINATED UNDER SECTION 7.3 OF THE LITURGY, AS VOTED BY THE COUNCIL. CONSUMERS ARE ADVISED TO STAY INDOORS FOR THEIR OWN SAFETY. DISCUSSION ON THIS MATTER IS DISCOURAGED."

On Sigma-6 Street, Sophie and her neighbours watched horrified as the helicopters arrived and began unwinding massive steel chains. The residents encircled the Tree's trunk, pressing themselves as close to it as they could. Others soon joined to form a growing protective mass. But it was not enough. The drones evaded them easily, threading the chains higher up the trunk and onto the larger branches. They flew back, pulling the chains tighter and tighter until...

"YOU-SA STOP DIS NARNSENSE – NOW!" A tinny, musical voice carried from somewhere up high. Everyone looked up in surprise. Even the drones' robotic operators momentarily slackened the chains.

"I SAY – STOP DIS NARNSENSE IM-ME-DIYAT-LY!" Old Ma Laurel, all eighty-odd years of her, had climbed onto one of the uppermost branches of the Tree, and was wagging her finger at the drone most directly in front of her.

"DIS TREE IS NAT YOURS TO DES-TROY. IT DOES NOT BELONG TO YOU-SA. IT DOES NAT BELONG TO A-NEE-WAN. LEAVE IT BE, EH!" With a roar of approval, the people below began to climb the Tree to join her. They clambered onto the branches, they hung from every part of the trunk, they pulled at the chains to disorientate the drones. Those left on the ground began to pass chainsaws and metal cutters upwards; others began to chant and sing in protest.

At this collective outpouring, the Tree absorbed the many tiny pieces of hidden selfless magic offered by each citizen of Lomah, and two curious things happened. First of all, the clouds suddenly parted. The sun's rays lit the city for the first time in hundreds of years, embracing the inhabitants with its dazzling, disorientating brilliance. The drones, however, could not cope. Overloaded by unknown visual data, they crashed – spiralling downwards in smoke.

Then, when Old Ma Laurel and the rest of the tree-climbers were safely back on ground, the Tree stretched upward as if inhaling and sent one final shudder into the earth below. Rippling across the city, under buildings, highways, parking lots and shopping malls, a monumental wave of energy travelled along the Tree's enormous and chaotic root system all the way to its tips – where it hit the Wall.

A deep CRACK resonated, followed by another, then another, and then a growing continuous rumble. To the sound of a thousand jubilant timpanis, the Wall – that had stood for longer than Lomah had allowed itself to remember – disintegrated into dust.

This was how the citizens of Lomah found themselves suddenly confronted with the mysterious world beyond the Wall. Face to face with the unknown, they could have found a million reasons to put the Wall right back up again. But now they were part of a conversation that could not stop, the threads of that magical blanket were already weaving a new story. So, together, they climbed out over the rubble and walked towards a future that they could write for themselves.

18
The Great Glass Stopper
Chris Nichols

The great glass stopper took one more turn. All around, fish of every colour looked on. What would the next moment bring?

The tank was old and wonderful. The carving, the glazing, the setting on the rich wood of the gold inlayed shelf: each part in its own way magnificent. The tank was home to a large tribe of fish from all corners of the world: some plain, some beautiful, some gentle, some frankly sharp finned and poisonous. They lived side by side in the tank and, somehow, it seemed to work.

All seemed to work until one day, with a splish and a splosh, a new fish appeared in their mix: a rare and exotic philibut, of a kind never before seen in the antique tank.

At first, the philibut lived gently among them, learning their names and their ways. Slowly though his exotic heritage began to cause ripples, and the other fish began to take notice. The philibut began to say some worrying things...

There was a rumour that the hand that fed the fish was ailing, the philibut said. Some of the fish nodded, and noticed that indeed, year upon year, the helpings were getting smaller.

We need new sources of food, said the philibut. I know of a great eastern land where fish food flows like water. We must turn our shoals to feed from a new direction. A new direction?... Many of the fish were sceptical, but more food would certainly be needed if the feeding hand was ailing. Who could argue?

The philibut began to tell another story. There was, he said, a Great Koi. And the Great Koi believed that all the fish should leave their antique home. The Great Koi had said that their beloved tank was too small, and that all the fish should swim together in one steam, in one greater ocean. Now this was very scary. The fish loved their tank, and some had swum hard against strong currents to come to lay their eggs there.

"Our tank is special," they said.

"Our water is different," some added.

"Some of the fish in the other streams and oceans can't even swim and have funny ways" others had heard.

But the philibut smiled and blew friendly bubbles. In the bubbles, the fish saw the hope of warmer waters and more food. They allowed the philibut to give one swift turn to the Great Glass Stopper that held their sacred waters safely in place.

After a while, the philibut led the fish to the far corner of the tank, where they found an old, old fish. "This is a wise and marvellous old fish," said the philibut, "and a trusted friend from many long ocean adventures."

The marvellous old fish flicked his tail into the sandy bottom and up spiralled a cloud of spinning sand.

"Look into the patterns," said the marvellous old fish. "See the future, search for it there."

The fish looked on, amazed. Some of them could see a future of food from the east. Some of them said that they saw the Great Koi beckoning them forwards. All agreed that the philibut had an interesting friend in the marvellous old fish and were more than ever keen to swim close behind him. Many were ready to set off for the future right there and then and began to ready themselves for a great adventure.

They encouraged the philibut to give the Great Glass Stopper one more turn. Now the stopper stood proud of the tank bottom: only one more twist remained and the adventure would begin.

As the great adventure came ever closer some of the fish became nervous.

"Will we be safe?" they asked.

"What will the water be like?" they said.

"Will we be eaten?" some worried.

The philibut called the whole tank together, and all the fish swam around in a great shoal, tails flicking, colours flashing. All trying to hear what the philibut had to say.

"I have spoken with the Great Koi," the philibut said, "and all is well."

There was a great bubbling of relief...

"The Great Koi has asked me to swim at the front, the very front of the great adventure... I will be with you as we join the streams and oceans," he said... "And all of our beloved water will go with us."

The fish swam gaily around, flashing their colours. They allowed the philibut to nudge the Great Glass Stopper so that almost all of it was now free.

A new day dawned and the philibut swam towards the Great Glass Stopper. The fish could see there would be no turning back now, the stopper was already too far out of the hole ever to go fully back. The philibut swam forward.

The great glass stopper took one more turn. All around, fish of all colours looked on: what would the next moment bring?

The Great Glass Stopper toppled sideward.

There was a moment of stillness.

There was a moment of calm.

And then a great sucking and pulling gripped the fish, as all of the water in the tank began to move with an insistent urging towards the hole where the Great Glass Stopper had been.

The fish swirled into the pipe. Round and around they went...

The pipe was not dark, but was a confusing array of patterns, colours... Which way was up, what was east, which way was West? Not one of the fish could tell. They simply swam on, swirling round and round in the current that ran away from their tank towards the streams and ocean.

Far behind in the empty tank lay the philibut. The exotic philibut, the friend of the marvellous old fish, the speaker with the Great Koi had overlooked one, and only one, thing. He was just the wrong shape to fit into the hole left by the Great Glass Stopper.

The philibut lay flapping on the bottom of the tank in the last pool of the remaining water.

"Everything will be alright," he flapped.

"Swim forward, swim, east!" he mouthed... "The search for the marvellous future goes on."

And the fish swam on, towards the ocean and the Great Koi.

Behind them some could still hear the philibut.

"Everything is going to be alright", he flapped.

19
The Town Musicians of Naarich

Bill McGuire

The New Year's Day storm was the last straw. It was the third occasion in less than six months that the salt pans had been laid waste, but this time there was no way back. The spume-laden winds had driven before them a massive surge that had overwhelmed the lagoons, destroyed the harvesting machinery and the warehouses and battered the workers shanty town into matchwood. More than half of the indentured labourers and their families had been killed, and those that remained were left with nothing but the sodden rags they stood up in.

The following morning a blazing sun in a blue, rain-washed, sky looked down on the small band of survivors called together by Mr John, the owner of the salt manufactory. Most were men. The women and children had been inside the shacks when the surge struck and few had survived. The men had been working on the pans, and although many had drowned, some had managed to make it to the safety of the great dunes that enclosed the evaporating lagoons.

There were about thirty survivors in all. They stood with their arms at their sides, several clutching the wide-brimmed hats worn as protection from the sun's enervating heat. They looked not at Mr John, but cast their eyes downwards, seemingly studying the debris-strewn sand.

Mr John cleared his throat. He was a fat man – a rare sight indeed in these times. The armpits of his safari jacket were marked by dark stains and he mopped his brow with a red silk handkerchief as the building heat nurtured sprouting beads of sweat. He had good news, he told them, from the upturned crate upon which he stood. They were free.

There was little reaction to the news. A few shuffled their feet, but they had learned to their cost never to speak in Mr John's presence. No-one even looked up. They kept their eyes downcast, occasionally sneaking a sideways glance at one of the cattle-prod wielding overseers who corralled the group. A sickly-looking child enveloped in the arms of an old man, squealed momentarily, but was calmed by the man's whispered endearments.

The sound of Mr John rapping his thigh with his silver-topped prod was the only sound that broke the silence. He seemed to be at a loss about what to do next. Then, when it became clear that his magnanimous gesture was to be greeted neither with enthusiasm nor – indeed – any sign at all, he gave a tight smile and signalled over the heads of the labourers to the overseers. Turning away from the gathering, he stepped down and waddled along the path through the dunes that led to the track where four battered jeeps were parked.

The overseers followed in single file, the last man walking backwards and pointing a machine pistol at the assembly until he disappeared from sight. There was a sound of clattering engine parts then, as the drivers started up the jeeps, and a savoury odour as the recycled cooking oil powered the vehicles forward.

No-one moved or spoke until the noise of the retreating jeeps had faded. Only then did a murmur of subdued conversation intrude upon the swashing sound of the distant waves. The assembly broke up. People formed small clumps that separated to make new associations that disbanded in turn; singletons bounced back and forth amongst the groups like atoms in a cloud of gas. Here and there – amidst the hubbub – individuals sat or stood; alone, friendless and bereft.

Lexy dragged his eyes from a bent old woman shivering beneath black rags despite the sun's heat. Husband and son taken by the surge, he had no doubt that Mr John's announcement had sounded the death knell for her and for many of those left behind. There had been no pity, no generosity of spirit, in his final act. It had been a strictly commercial decision. The frequent storms had simply become too much, the near-continuous repairing and rebuilding making the manufactory unsustainable. He had others – better placed, more sheltered from the periodic surges. He would expand these to make up for the loss of this one. With no work, no shelter and no food, most of the survivors would likely starve, but that wasn't his concern. It was nothing personal. Business was business.

'So, what now boss?'

Lexy turned and looked down at an upturned face, furrowed and burnt nut-brown by the sun. The glittering black eyes looked out from deep pits of shadow, the small mouth partly open in a toothless gape. The tiny man barely came up to Lexy's waist, but he was almost as broad as he was tall, and the arms that sprouted through ragged holes in his shirt were muscled like a wrestlers. In his right hand, he clutched a rough-made flute – now his only possession.

Lexy shrugged, then raised his eyes again to scan the horizon, as if looking for inspiration.

'There's nothing for us here now, Prince. We have to go.'

Maybe the dwarf had acquired his name because he was the exact opposite of what a Prince might be expected to look like, but nobody had dared ask. Now he nodded at Lexy's edict and signalled to a man standing nearby, a young woman sitting cross-legged on the sand at his feet. The woman stood and they both came over. The man was called Pop – also for reasons unknown. Fair of skin and red of hair, he was not designed for working long hours in the sun. He had a large, bulbous, nose from which, periodically, flakes of burned epidermis drifted like dandruff.

His skin was pale, but across his cheeks and arms, freckles had merged to form patches of near-continuous red. His flaming hair, shot with grey, was long, but tied up in a bun and stuffed beneath the wide-brimmed hat he could never afford to be without. The matching straggly beard reached almost to his waist. He was extremely tall, and thin to the point of emaciation.

The woman had no name, or at least had never admitted or answered to one. She was half Pop's age and might have been his daughter, though she wasn't. She was gamine and deeply tanned. Well muscled and sinewy, she looked out on the world through bright blue eyes set in a long, thin, face and slitted against the sun. Both wore the standard knee-length ragged trews of the salt pan labourer. Neither wore footwear of any sort. Like all who worked the evaporation lagoons, their feet were hardened almost to stone by the salt. The man carried a small drum, made of skin drawn across a framework of driftwood. The woman grasped a hand-crafted fiddle and bow that had seen far better days. The pair joined Prince and all three waited patiently in Lexy's shadow for him to speak.

He was something of an oddity amongst the labourers, having come to the camp as a youth, traded for hack silver by an old couple at their wit's end. By virtue of his experience of the world beyond the camp, Lexy was venerated by those who had known nothing else. Despite the frugal diet, he was a huge man, which attracted a mix of respect and awe from the labourers, but also – inevitably – the attention and hostility of the overseers.

In order to survive, Lexy had learned early on to keep his head down and to say as little as possible. Prince had been instrumental, taking him under his wing and tempering teenaged anger and angst that could quite easily have seen him strung up within days of arrival. It was Prince who inducted Lexy into the ways of the camp; what to do and what not to do; who was trouble and who wasn't. As memories of his father faded, it was Prince who took his place. Now well into his third decade, it was to Prince that Lexy owed everything.

He looked down now with fondness on the little man and nodded to Pop and his nameless companion. He was glad they had all survived. Music had brought them together and kept them together. During the blistering nights, when sleep was impossible, they had played to keep everyone's spirits up and hope alive. Hope in what, no-one was sure, but the music made everyone feel better – at least for a time.

'There's a town not too far from here. I remember we stopped off there before...' Lexy struggled for the words.

'...before I came. Naarich, I think it's called.' He hefted his pipes in one hand. 'I thought maybe we could play. For food like.'

Pop looked less than convinced and made a face. He worked his cracked lips – as if preparing them – before speaking 'How far?'

Lexy frowned, trying to recall memories that he had intentionally buried deep. 'Three days walk – maybe four.'

Pop worked his lips again. 'And what do we eat? How do we feed ourselves on the journey?'

Lexy shrugged, but had no answer. Prince, ever supportive, came to his aid.

'There's no food here either. Stay if you wish and starve slowly, or come with us and try your luck. There is no other choice.'

The girl touched Pop's arm and he bent down so she could whisper in his ear. She was a marvel on her fiddle, but never spoke out loud or to anyone other than Pop.

Pop stood upright. He still didn't look pleased, but he nodded. 'We will come.'

The four wound their way through the other survivors, some still talking quietly in groups, others sitting or lying on the sand. No-one took any notice as they headed towards the path through the dunes that led to the track, and they didn't look back.

The battlements of the cloud castles were bruised purple and black, heralding the evening downpour that helped dissipate the day's grinding heat and humidity. Before them, they watched – mouths open – as the blinding light of the setting sun at their backs bounced off a wall of water surging westwards. They stood at the southern edge of a finger of the sea that pointed far inland. Long ago, when the heat came and the seas rose up, the salt water overwhelmed the meres and freshwater lakes that had occupied the subdued topography and now the sea reached almost as far as Naarich. The tidal bore was commonplace to those who knew it, roaring inland twice a day. But to Lexy and his companions, it was something marvellous and unexplained, and they followed its course until it merged into the gloom of the coming dusk.

Lexy moved off then, the others trudging behind. It was their second day on the road and they were bone-tired. They had kept to the track that followed the southern edge of the narrow bay. Even so, the going had been hard, run-off from the daily rainstorms chopping the surface into a mosaic of deep fissures that turned ankles and gouged shins. They were famished too. Some small, wrinkled, fruit, scavenged from a stand of moribund orange trees had kept them going and accumulated rainwater had held thirst at bay. But they desperately needed something more to give them the energy to keep moving.

They had encountered no-one on the track, a shoal of small fishing boats flitting past at the height of the previous evening's rainstorm providing the only sign of life. It was a surprise, therefore, when – as thunder crashed at their backs and the skies opened – the outline of a building emerged from the rainy murk, the flicker of candlelight in the windows. More often than not, people meant bad news, so the four drew closer warily. A small copse of stunted palms to one side offered shelter and they made for this.

The building had two stories – almost unknown these days – and was well made. The walls were built from chalk blocks and must have been centuries old. They had been repaired in places and the original roof had been replaced by sheets of corrugated iron, but the work had been well done. The place looked watertight and welcoming. While the others crouched beneath the dripping branches, Prince crept closer until he could steal a glance through one of the downstairs windows. After a time, he scuttled on to the next, then vanished around a corner. Minutes later, he reappeared, having circumnavigated the building, and made a dash for the trees, scuttling in a low crouch through the deluge. He looked excited.

'Mr John and three of the overseers.' He paused to wipe at his dripping face. 'There are two jeeps parked round the back. The others must have gone on ahead.'

Lexy and Pop were startled by the news and the girl made whimpering noises. She had been a favourite of Mr John a while back, before she had bitten a chunk out of his arm. They had staked her out on the sand then, dawn 'til dusk – no water. She had been lucky to survive. Very lucky. Why Mr John would stop here they couldn't imagine and they wasted a few minutes discussing possibilities, before Lexy raised both hands in exasperation.

'It doesn't matter why he's here. Question is, what are we going to do about it?'

John Thaxton blew out the candle on the windowsill and peered out; long, pointed nose almost touching the chill glass. It was nearly dark and the rain had at last stopped its mind-numbing clattering on the iron-clad roof. Now the water that had fallen was evaporating fast from the hot ground. It formed a thick mist that drifted in from the salt marshes bordering the south side of the bay, hugging the ground and swirling around the building. Mr John shivered. It wasn't cold, but this place gave him the creeps. He was familiar with the tales of the dead, whose spirits haunted the marshes when the moon was full. He didn't believe them, of course, but, well..... you could never be really sure could you?

He turned back to the dimly lit room as if for reassurance. Two of his men were sprawled on battered, overstuffed, chairs; two asleep and snoring, the other fiddling with the broken strap of his machine pistol. Mr. John grimaced. He hated the place and was desperate to get out, but it served a purpose. His grimace turned to an indulgent smile as he thought of the wheeling and dealing he had done there over the years; the money he had made; the people he had screwed over.

He turned back to the window and squinted hopefully into the blackness. Where the fuck was the Colonel? He was a full day late now. It just wasn't good enough. Not good enough at all. If it hadn't been for the prospect of closing the biggest deal of his life, he would have been out of there long ago. No-one made him twiddle his thumbs like this. No-one. Then again, the Colonel wasn't no-one. He was someone –

someone big. Control of the salt market in Lundun had made him unimaginably rich and immensely powerful, and Mr John wanted a bit of that. If he could get the Colonel to take his salt he was made; guaranteed a market big enough to take everything he could produce and more.

Delusions of grandeur were beginning to blossom in his head, when he became aware of lights outside. His first thought was that they were headlights, that the Colonel had come at last. Excitement began to build, then turned quickly to anxiety as the mist parted to unmask a baleful, yellow moon and – out on the waters of the bay – it's fluttering reflection. At the same moment, a blood-curdling wail sounded close by. On and on it went, echoing out across the water. Mr John stood transfixed, the hairs on the back of his neck standing to attention. Behind him, he could hear his men scrabbling for their weapons and turning saw terror in their eyes. They were local lads and none too bright. He could see that they knew the stories, been raised on them, had swallowed them wholesale.

Just then, the wail sounded again, this time joined by an awful screeching, like the death throws of a stuck piglet. The men panicked then, grabbing their guns and making for the door. Mr. John crossed the room in an attempt to head them off, blocking the doorway and putting out an arm. They stopped in their tracks, unsure of what to do.

'Lads, lads. Calm down. It's nothing – just the wind.' He didn't believe it himself, so didn't hold out much hope that they would. Then there came another sound. This time a slow thump – thump, thump – thump, thump – thump, like the steady pounding of a funeral drum. It was the last straw. The man in front yelled in horror and swung a ham-sized fist at Mr John's face, which knocked him to the ground and had him seeing stars. In seconds, they were through the door and into the hallway. Mr John shook his head to clear it. At the same time, he became aware of a ghostly ululation, a pulsing cadence that chilled him to the core, and which went on and on. He swallowed hard, rationality beginning to fade, dread building.

Then the sound was drowned out by the noise of an engine turning over, and he struggled to rise. He still felt groggy, and managed only to drag himself up onto all fours, head drooping between his arms, belly touching the floor, blood from his shattered nose dripping onto the threadbare carpet.

'No! Lads. Don't leave me.' He shouted at the floor. His throat was dry and his voice weak. There was the slamming of doors, then the crunching of gears and a grating screech as one of the jeeps made off. Mr. John hauled himself to his feet, one arm holding onto the door jamb for support. He was dripping with cold sweat and his chins wobbled as he cried out again in despair.

'Noooo.....Please. Come back!' The screech of another engine pushed to its limits announced the departure of the second jeep. Then there was silence.

Mr John slumped to the ground, sobbing, the tears mingling with the dribble of blood from his nose.

For a long time, he sat on the floor, unmoving. Then, aware that the sounds of the tormented souls had ceased, he pulled himself upright once more and stumbled into the hall. The outside door was open and, uncertain of what to do next, he ventured – tentatively – out into the night.

The moon, was high in the sky now, casting the landscape into a mosaic of black and silver. Mr John's attention was attracted to the silhouette of a large boulder a few yards away. He didn't remember seeing it when they arrived. When the boulder moved and resolved itself into a tiny man, he opened his mouth to scream. But is was a sound that never came. A thin but sinewy arm reached from behind and a hand clamped over his mouth, pulling his head back. The slim-bladed knife slipped easily between his ribs and into his heart, which fibrillated momentarily, then stopped.

The girl released her grip, stepped back and let the lifeless body of Mr John slump to the ground. Prince joined her then and they stood for a moment looking down at the pudgy face, glistening in the moonlight. Then the girl hawked and spat on the bloodied corpse.

The melancholy skirl of pipes greeted the appearance of the sun. A gusting breeze carried the wistful notes far across the sparkling waters of the bay, piquing the interest of a black-sailed trading wherry that came close to the shore, its occupants waving a greeting before heading on down the coast. Lexy had parked himself on a small rock to watch the sun come up. Now he took the reed from his mouth and turned as the others came to join him. In their hands, they carried their musical instruments. No-one spoke and for a time they just watched the wherry and kept their own counsel. Eventually, Prince broke the silence.

'So. Do we stay or do we go?'

Lexy grinned at him. 'Well, there are four walls and a roof, and there's food and water. I'm happy with that.' Prince nodded his agreement. Lexy squinted up at Pop's piebald face and waited. Pop was working his mouth, preparing his reply, when the girl plucked at his sleeve and he bent to catch her whisper, then straightened. His face became distorted then, and Lexy realised, after a moment, that he was smiling. 'She likes it here and so do I. We vote we stay.'

Lexy beamed back, 'Then, my friends', he said, turning again to look out over the sparkling blue waters of the bay: 'Naarich must wait a little longer to savour our particular talents.'

Author's note:
With a bit of a nod to the popular fairy tale *The Town Musicians of Bremen*, retrieved and recorded by the Brothers Grimm and first published in *Grimms' Fairy Tales* in 1819.

20

The Woman on the Road

Peter Spooner

Once upon a time there was an old woman who lived beside a long, long road. The road had countless branches, and it connected many cities and situations of all kinds.

Everyone used the road; it was the only way to get anywhere worth going, to see anyone worth seeing. Intense, focused types who hoped they were 'going places' used it especially often. Sometimes, they even got to those places. But, more often than not, travellers only made it to some lonely halfway stop from which they struggled to move on, chained by circumstance, bright distraction, the price of fuel, weighed down by trinkets from the many roadside attractions. Some unfortunates made it only a short distance before they were choked almost to death by the dust, forced to give up on their dreams, or crushed under the wheels of those coming on fast behind.

The old lady who lived beside the road used it to fetch her groceries. Each day she walked out along her garden path, turned right, and went slowly onwards, mile by mile. Whenever someone came up behind her, she would kindly step aside and let them pass by. After all, she was getting so slow, no longer in the race, and the youngsters all had flashy fast cars or buzzing scooters. In fact, almost everyone on the road went faster than the old woman, and she had to step aside rather a lot.

Sometimes, the people who went past would slow down for a second, maybe even shout 'HI THERE!' One or two might ask her for directions, but all she could do was point vaguely into the distance, trying to be helpful; but she knew the right way to follow no better than anybody else.

However, not many slowed down – they didn't have the time – and mostly they kept right on going by, having discovered new-fangled means of direction that excused talk with local nobodies. The old woman didn't mind too much; so long as the youngsters knew where they were going, she could be happy for them.

One day she heard a car coming up fast behind and stepped off the road and sat on a rock to rub her feet. The car hurtled past, kicking up a great cloud of dust and dirt as it went. Some of the dirt got into the shoe she had just taken off, and she shook it out angrily. But then she thought, *they might be a little selfish, but it's not their fault. I hope they get to wherever it is they're going.* Crouching on the rock, the old woman began to look something like a rock herself, so that many more young travellers went by without knowing she was there at all. Finally she re-buckled her shoe, stood up feeling like a tree unbending, and went, aching, on her way.

The next week the road was busier, and the old woman sat on the rock for a bit longer than was usual.

There were more cars on the road, so that instead of walking along its smoothed surface she had to beat a path along the verge, where rough clods of earth prodded at her feet and sharp stones bit into her heels. Her feet were terribly sore, but she had to fetch the groceries.

Sitting on the rock she began to resent the traffic. *They should introduce a law or something*, she thought; *get folks to slow down a little*. But she didn't want to stop people going about their business, business that she felt must be very important because she couldn't think of another reason for their rushing about all the time. Eventually she went back on her way, but it was hard, and when she got to the store most of her usual groceries had run out, so she sighed with disappointment and made do with the slim pickings that remained.

The next week, the road was even busier than before, and the old woman got to the rock and she stayed there, not feeling able to go on, or to go back. Her legs were shaking, and she breathed heavily, and it seemed that her lungs were sucking all the exhaust fumes out of the air. *Well I don't know what to do now*, she thought. *I don't like to bother anyone, but I do wish someone would stop and help me*. But no one seemed to notice her, and she sat there for a long time and felt very alone.

Eventually a car pulled over onto the verge and a family got out, a mother, a father, and a tearful little girl with pigtails and a bright blue dress. But it was clear that they had not stopped on account of the old woman. 'HOW CAN YOU HAVE GOT US LOST?' the Mother was shouting.

'I WAS TRYING MY BEST!' replied the Father. 'IF THE DAMN SATNAV HADN'T GONE AND BUSTED, I WOULDN'T HAVE HAD TO TRY AND FIND MY OWN WAY. WHY DIDN'T YOU KEEP THE ROAD ATLAS?'

'EVERYONE SAID WE DIDN'T NEED THEM ANY MORE. HOW WAS I TO KNOW ANY BETTER?'

And so they went on, while the old woman sat and watched and said nothing. Meanwhile, forgotten and unnoticed, the little girl wandered shyly over and plucked at the old woman's skirts.

The old woman looked down in surprise at the girl's tear-stained face and said, 'There there sweetheart. What's the matter?'

'We're lost,' sobbed the little girl, 'and Mummy and Daddy get angry and shout all the time.'

'Well now. Everyone gets lost sometimes, and I'm sure your Mummy and Daddy will make it up very soon.' The old woman put her arm around the girl to comfort her, and the girl cuddled gratefully by her side. She curled there tightly, and slowly the shouting faded from her thoughts.

When the girl had stopped crying, she asked – for she was a curious creature – 'What are you doing sitting here all on your own?'

'I'm sitting here because my feet hurt, and I don't think I can even get to the shops today, and maybe not even home neither.'

'What were you going to buy?' asked the little girl, who loved shops of every kind.

'Oh, only food and things. Little bits I need to get by,' answered the old woman.

They sat together for a while, the little girl describing all the things that she wanted to be when she grew up, the old woman nodding along but thinking how unlikely it all was. Eventually the shouting stopped, reverting to a sullen, grumpy silence.

The adults paced about for a while. Then the mother called out 'SOPHIE! Sophie darling? TIME TO GO!'

The little girl looked at the old woman. 'I'll ask my daddy if you can go with us', she said kindly. The old woman smiled down at her and touched her cheek with one careful finger.

'That would be awful kind of you,' she said, 'but I wouldn't want to make any trouble. I'll be happy to sit here just a bit longer. Only… I only wish I had a nicer view than that goddamning dusty road all the time.'

The little girl laughed at the old woman's language and said: 'That's silly. You don't have to look at the road at all. Why don't you just turn round and look over there?' She took the old woman's hands and helped her shuffle slowly around on the rock, putting her back firmly to the road. And when the old woman raised her head once more and looked, she saw before them the green ground sloping away downwards between hills rising steep and high on either side, thick with trees of many colours.

And not so far away, at the bottom of the valley, the land sank beneath the blue waves of the sea, lit in a long streak by the bright, clear sun, and the shining waters stretched out and out and out; and out again until they were lost to sight over the edge of the world. 'My oh my!', said the old woman, and she sighed with joy, forgetting the cracks in her heels, the dust in her lungs, the blaring of horns behind her. 'I'd forgotten how beautiful the world could be.'

'SOPHIE!' called the Mother once more. 'I WON'T TELL YOU AGAIN!'

The girl was reluctant. 'Can we take this nice old lady with us Mummy? She wants to go to the shops to get some food and things.'

'Don't be so silly dear,' said the mother. 'We're not carrying giant rocks like that around in the car just for fun.' She said this because she could not see the old woman, who had gone out of her world. 'And besides the supermarket is *really* out of our way, and your Daddy thinks he's found a shortcut to Victorville.'

'I'm sorry', said the little girl quietly to the old woman, squeezing her hand. 'I've got to go or they'll get angry and mean again. When I'm older, I'll come and find you and we can play together. I know lots of fun games.'

'That would be very nice dear,' said the old woman quietly, but she was distracted by the sight below her. She thought she remembered something like it from a very, very long time ago, when she was young, when the road was only a little winding thing. She felt her soul slipping slowly out into the valley, fair feet stepping out onto the welcoming earth. 'Promise me you'll be good now,' she murmured. And then she was quiet, and heard only the wind in the trees, and the rushing of the bright water far away as she went down to meet them.

'I promise,' said the little girl sadly, and she let the old woman's hand fall. But where it fell it touched a flower, clinging on to life at the edge of the world. And then the girl decided that one day she would grow to be a gardener, and that she would make all the world just as beautiful as her memory of this place. She wanted to stay longer, to reach out and touch the sea, but her mother was shouting again. So she turned reluctantly and ran to re-join her family, and the road.

21

The Loves of Wolfdog Aurora

Lisa Rabanal

One beast and only one is the true enemy of those that used to howl in the woods by night. The human is carnivore incarnate. As cunning as they are greedy, once they've had the taste of flesh, nothing else will do.

And, oh furry one, for beauties like you who are not good to eat, they'll have other plans. They trap you for your pelt, they hunt you for their sport, they'll kill you out of mean-spiritedness. They may befriend you, but beware, they're sure to cage you, or otherwise use you. Fear and flee the human oh gentle wolf, for, worst of all, the human may be more than they seem.

Once upon a memory, in a land far across the Atlantic Ocean, the Queen of the wolfdogs, a matriarch named Bella, gave birth to her seventh litter. This time was like any other, and the puppies, except the smallest and least likely to thrive, were taken from her, never to be seen again. The silver-grey female pup, Aurora, the seventh in the litter, was strong, a survivor. A substantial deposit had been paid for one just like her, even before her birth.

Now, at the beginning of this tale, Aurora is curled calmly at the end of a battered leather sofa, facing a flat screen TV. Her nose is tucked into her tail, her yellow eyes are closed, and her little rounded body rises with her soft breath. She does not know the lore of her ancestors and has had no real reason to dread the human companions who bottle-fed her and packed her into a crate and brought her all the way to a small European island.

Nor does she fear the new human family with whom she finds herself. The humans have dissimilar interests to her on the whole, but they have access to plentiful food and share some of the tastiest, smelliest, meatiest items from their cupboards. They are willing to play, sometimes. And the smallest one curls up with her on the sofa bed, a substitute for the littermates she never got to know.

Aurora is just fifteen weeks old, but the hopes and dreams of the human family rest on this little princess. She is an F3 hybrid, part wolf, part dog. Imported from America, she is rare and valuable. Her pups, like her, will be hard to manage, but expensive to secure. Aurora is the golden goose, cash cow, wolf dog.

Time passes. Aurora grows. Her early passions for chewing electric cables, digging up floor tiles, and pulling down curtains are replaced by calmer pursuits. She catches frogs or pigeons in the garden, and more commonly, spends her time following the small human boy who feeds her biscuits. When she was younger, she left the house, accompanied, a few times, but now the humans find her too strong, and are scared of 'what might happen' should she meet one of the other dogs on the estate.

Her world, then, is small: three rooms, shared with humans, and the fenced garden beyond. She now knows to urinate and defecate neatly outdoors, and in so doing communicates with the free creatures of the night so that they might know the boundaries of her outside domain, and share her reverence of favourite bowls and bones. Within the house, she sheds her wintery fur coat, and generously perfumes the environment with her damp paws and musky glands.

There are warm, faintly mud-stained, hollows on the cushions where her body lays, and, whenever she is left she marks the occasion by scratching wood and chewing upholstery.

'This bloody puppy has ruined my house!' exclaims a human. Aurora cares not – she assumes these territories to be her own.

When her first blood arrives, she accepts the flow with equanimity. Although usually defined by carefree untidiness, she meticulously and regularly licks herself clean. She surprises the humans by refusing to come in at night for a few days, instead, alert in the backyard, she spends the early hours of the morning staring into the distance, occasionally uttering a mournful howl.

Six months later, when the blood comes again, the humans are resolved that the time has come to find Aurora a suitor. This first goes by the name of Thor.

He arrives early one afternoon, thunderous indeed, living, breathing, furrily handsome; a Czech wolfdog of apparently impeccable pedigree.

'Lovely bitch.' said Thor's human handler, visually appraising Aurora. 'She'll take to him no trouble.'

Aurora is not so sure about whoever, whatever, this alien is upon her territory. As Thor approaches, the fur that runs along her backbone stands on end, her tail stiffens to a warning pole.

'Get on Thor,' grumbles the visiting human, pulling the big dog forward by his collar and lead 'Don't be a wuss. Goin' to let a girl scare you?'

It happens much too fast for slow-processing human eyes and minds to properly comprehend. Aurora spins and grabs. And Thor lies on the floor, beneath her paws, her teeth on his neck. It takes three of the humans to pull Aurora away and release the big male.

'Bloody hell. That dog's dangerous, you want to have her muzzled, mate,' yells the man with Thor, as he drags the big dog back to the car parked out front.

The seasons pass. When the bleeding comes again, it is time for Aurora to meet her second suitor. This one does not court Aurora within the confines of her homely prison garden. For the first time as an adult, Aurora leaves her home and travels by car to an unfamiliar building that smells of fear, and blood, and of the kinds of creatures that Aurora has never met but that she knows are fit to chase.

These scents are masked with a heavy overlay of antiseptic. The floor is slippery and the waiting room is narrow. Aurora takes over the space. Her humans use new tones of voice in this public place, enunciating more clearly than usual, and appear slightly exasperated, as though Aurora's failure to understand things they have never before asked of her, is somehow her own shortcoming.

'Lie down, lie down,' they plead, uselessly.

Aurora strains at the end of her leash, pulling towards the hiss of a caged cat, and the exciting bug-eyed snuffle of a pug on a woman's lap.

She is hastily led to another room and two of them heft her on to a table. A muzzle is placed over her nose and a chain attached to her collar so that she is now held in position via a hook on the ceiling. A white-coated man appears to be in charge. He carefully extracts a vial, labeled 'dog semen,' into a syringe and then into a tube. Anxiously, the humans gather at Aurora's rear end. The white-coated one inserts a straw deep inside her and the precious contents of the tube are squeezed into her body.

Immediately outside the vets, Aurora squats. 'Don't do that!' the humans implore. But it's too late, she urinates calmly and at length, until satisfied that the alien juice has been purged from her body.

Five weeks later, Aurora makes her second trip to the antiseptic room. She is again muzzled, and lifted to a table where she is held in position lying on her back. Her belly is shaved, a cold gel applied, and a rounded probe moved up and down over the newly bare area. The vet stares ruefully at a screen in front of him. 'Sorry, nothing there, I'm afraid. She's not pregnant.'

Aurora's third suitor arrives long before the next blood. He has been summoned hastily for this wolfy girl who has learned to tame and tire her humans.

Aurora is large, but can melt into shadows. She watches as the front door is opened to reveal the tall, lean, human stranger, clad in trainers and lycra. Silently she pads forwards and sniffs the air. Among other notes, Aurora detects fresh perspiration, newly mowed grass, and a pocketful of liver treats. The handsome stranger bends slowly down to greet her, and she licks the salty sweat from his face. He tastes just right. Ambrosial.

'I've been running,' he says with a grin, 'fancy coming with me next time?' Aurora likes his soft, friendly, tone, which she finds euphonious.

The stranger raises himself up to speak with Aurora's human.

'Such a shame you can't keep her. You must be upset – she's beautiful. But I promise I'll give her a good home. Just lost my old boy Sam, I know my way round dogs.'

'Well, yeah. That's good mate. She just wants a bit of training. Worth thousands, but we're only looking at a monkey for her. High content wolfdog, this one. You can see she's worth it.'

'£500? The ad said free to a good home. Sorry, maybe I misunderstood something.' He imperceptibly makes a move backwards.

Aurora is watching intently. She turns, snuffles about in the dirty box at the back of the hallway, and delicately pulls out a seldom-used leash. Her lead between her teeth, she returns to the stranger, and butts his hand with her nose.

He looks at her, surprised and flattered.

She returns the gaze. Smitten, he marvels how unusual and beautiful are her amber eyes with their white lashes and lining of kohl black. He has the uncanny sensation that she can read his mind and find his soul.

Tenderly, the stranger scratches behind Aurora's ears, and, shaking his head and already reaching for his phone, asks: 'Bank transfer alright?'

Aurora is still and calm as the stranger affixes the lead to her collar and invites her to step out of the door by his side.

'Get her spayed, mate. I haven't had a chance, but you know, best thing to do,' is the parting shot from the one who has tried to control her since a pup.

'Of course,' says the stranger, glancing hastily over his shoulder, as the wolfdog forcefully tugs him forward. Aurora doesn't look back once. Her ears are erect, her tail is high, she is ready for adventures new. She was never just somebody's breeding bitch.

Author's note:
Inspired by the wonderful, feminist, wolfy tales in Angela Carter's *Bloody Chamber* (1979). The resemblance of any character to our Northern Inuit dog, Luna, is not coincidental.

22
Tipping Points
David Cross

Showing no outward signs of anxiety, the Directors of Finance, Strategic Development and Communications wait, while the *Vice Chancellor* takes a sip of coffee and looks out of the boardroom window. It is the first week of the new term, and like the heavy sky, the mood is electric. Yet although the quadrangle below him is alive with people, he can't identify any particular direction or purpose in their movement.

Gazing down at the crowd, he remembers his own student days. It's funny how things turn out, he reflects. After graduating, he rather drifted into the corporate sector, and although he had done well during some rather turbulent years, he'd been delighted when an executive recruitment agency approached him with an opportunity to lead a university. At interview, the panel had welcomed his proposal to build a lasting legacy, and now, as part of his ambitious programme of expansion and internationalization, he is about to make a decision on a new flagship building project.

He moves to bite a fingernail, but returns his hand to his pocket. Although the expansion would make his university the largest in the sector, it would mean taking on one of the largest debts in the history of higher education. However, he thought, as long as the international student market remains buoyant, and there is a favourable outcome to the pensions dispute, everyone can relax...

**

The flow of people entering the college building slows, while the *Security Guard* carefully checks every photo ID. He looks each person in the eye, and then smiles, a personal interaction that eases the task for all concerned. Appointed to a temporary posting, to cover while technical issues with the university's new automated entry system are being resolved, he is keen to make a good impression, which he hopes will lead to more regular employment with the agency.

Looking at this year's new faces, he wonders how much getting into university is down to having the money and contacts, and how much it is about hard work and talent. Music drifts in from the student café nearby, and he recognizes a Balearic beat from his days on the club scene. A musician and DJ himself, he is proud of his youngest daughter's joyful creativity and commitment to environmental causes. He is hoping to persuade her to go to art school next year, but struggling to convince himself that the debt will be an investment in her future.

Suddenly, a gust of wind blows through the corridor, and the heavy door at the end slams shut.

**

Always keen to focus on the positives, the *Catering Manager* tells herself that, in a way, it was lucky that the meat and dairy refrigerators had broken down during the heatwaves over the summer, when most of the students were away, rather than now.

Anyway, she's glad to have solved that problem, and having finally sorted out the invoice and paperwork, she takes her time to carefully display the new certificate announcing that she and her team have been awarded a national gold standard for sustainable catering. She's especially proud that the panel commended her work sourcing locally produced beef from animals, reared with high standards of animal welfare. Hearing a clatter and a loud rustling from out by the bin store, she stares as large sheets of packaging waste from the recent delivery whirl high in the air, almost as though caught up in a tornado. She calls to one of the staff to clear it up, and returns to planning the next steps moving forward. Could responding to the petition from the student vegan society demanding a plant-based menu wait, she wonders, until she has banned plastic straws from the canteen?

**

Switching his phone to silent, and turning down the sound on his computer to stop the chimes announcing each new email, the *Director of Estates and Operations* breathes a sigh, and closes his eyes. Outside, the wind is picking up, and the branch of a tree scrapes and taps almost frantically at the windowpane. In a moment, he will have to begin the task of ranking competing bids from companies for contracts to supply the university with services worth many millions of pounds.

With so many initiatives, developments and changing requirements impacting on everything from IT and communications, to security, waste disposal and even student accommodation, the possibility of outsourcing facilities management is becoming, let's say, more than appealing. A few years ago, when the students campaigned for fossil fuel divestment, energy procurement looked set to be a hot potato, and although the Executive had eventually pledged to divest one or two percent, it was something of a relief when the activists graduated and moved on.

But with increasing media coverage of extreme weather events around the world, and climate rebels taking to the streets, maybe it's time, he now thinks, to move this issue up the to-do list. Which deliverable should he prioritize – that academic's proposal for a research project to develop a distributed solar energy co-operative, or reviewing the energy procurement contract? Combining the two could open a can of worms.

**

The café is crowded and noisy with people talking excitedly about a major rally, but the *New Student* doesn't recognise anyone. She checks her smartphone, scrolling through "welcome" messages from the university's International Office, the timetable from her course tutor, and an offer of advice from her bank on managing compulsive spending. She won't be needing that kind of advice any time soon – besides, coming to university should be a chance to spread her wings. But it's definitely time to reply to those messages from her parents, as they seem anxious to know that she has made it safely from the airport and to hear if the apartment is OK. They're so caring and generous, yet their constant attentiveness sometimes adds to the pressure to succeed.

Here's a message about special deals on flights... The mid-term break isn't too far off, so maybe she could surprise them with a trip back home. On the other hand, her timetable includes a collaborative project, and a European city break might help her make new friends and broaden her horizons. She looks up from her phone to find herself facing a gender-fluid student in homemade clothes and an amazing tattoo. They hand her a weird-looking leaflet announcing a global climate emergency, smile and ask her name.

**

Feeling a slight pain in her lower back, the *Administrator* adjusts her new chair for optimum posture at the keyboard, and glances around at her surroundings with a sense of relief at having coped with the office move over the summer. Her vacation had been a washout, with floods at the airport delaying her departure, and the hotel barely up to speed after the recent forest fires. But to be fair, following the major restructure, she is lucky to have a job to come back to, when quite a few colleagues have moved on to pastures new. Her Line Manager has tasked her to deal with the backlog of expenses claims that built up when Central Services rolled out the new business system during the annual leave period, so she has a more than full workload.

On top of that, she's just received an email pleading for a late item to be added to the committee agenda. Skimming briskly over the message, she sees it's a proposal to review the university travel policy, with the introduction of a new points-based system, and something about whether carbon footprinting should include "radiative forcing". Fully updating all the documents now would make her late for her yoga class, so for the time being she can pop the item in under "Any Other Business".

**

In over 15 years in the job, *the Technician* couldn't remember a more spectacular mountain of wreckage: good planed timber, particle board, paint, electrical cables, plaster, steel, copper, plastics, textiles and glass. All left behind by the graduating students when they disappeared after their degree shows. He doesn't blame them, though – with rack rents and the sky-high price of food, he can see that they need to cut costs and move on to find work as fast as possible. Here and now, Health & Safety regs dictate that the material all has to be quickly cleared away, and a tight turnaround between courses leaves precious little time for separating and sorting. So the mixed material gets dumped in countless skips and driven away in diesel trucks to the landfill site. Criminal, really. But as a member of the University Sustainability Committee, he's sharing ideas with colleagues and students for reducing the environmental impact of the workshops.

Who could say which is more important, he wonders: helping the designers avoid "monstrous hybrid" materials, transitioning to solvent-free screenprinting, or reducing the energy consumption of the ceramics kilns? He feels an unusual change in the air pressure, and listens anxiously to what sounds like the old flue stack to the air filtration system being buffeted in the gale. For weeks, he'd been meaning to replace the filter above the sawing and sanding machines, but now he can only watch as the ducting rattles loose, the used filter unit hits the fan, and the workshop starts to fill with a cloud of semi-hazardous dust.

**

The break seems to have come and gone in a flash; the stormy sky looks not so much like the end of summer as the end of the world. Perching at a hot desk to go through her email, the *Academic* is daunted by the sheer number of messages in her in-tray, many of which seem calculated to increase her irritation at the encroaching bureaucracy, and her anger reignites at the transformation of higher education into a tangle of commerce and surveillance.

Even the once-reassuring prospect of retirement seems increasingly unsettled, with continuing machinations around the University's Pension Scheme raising the prospect of another strike. How much longer can the pension remain sustainable, when there is no incentive for junior colleagues on precarious contracts to join the scheme? And with the divestment movement gaining strength, how will the fund cope when its fossil fuel investments become stranded assets? Despite petitions and reasoned argument, the pension fund managers have been less than forthcoming about investments in opencast coal mines and tar sands on the lands of First Nation Peoples, which casts an uncomfortable shadow over her new seminar series on Decolonization in Visual Culture.

Outside, lightning cracks the concrete sky, and a power outage plunges the room into darkness. Her pulse quickens and her pupils dilate, but she quickly gathers her composure. Hopefully, IT Services have fitted surge protectors, so she shouldn't have lost any data. But when the lights don't come back on, she moves away from the computer, opens the window, and hears the crowd in the courtyard below break into song.

A great peal of thunder rolls and tumbles across the city, then white noise fills the air as hailstones knock leaves and now twigs off the trees. Alarms sound and branches crack in the wild wind, and people run for cover as the downpour begins.

23

No More Worlds to Conquer

Corrina Cordon

A long time past, or perhaps a long time future, a King sat in his palace, surveyed the magnificence around him and wept. A solitary banquet sat before him, gold plates laden with food on a table of exquisite rose marble. This, in turn, stood on a floor of highly polished wood, covered with intricately woven rugs of silk and wool depicting fantastical creatures frolicking in wild meadows, faces shining with bliss.

The walls of the great hall were hung with a thousand mirrors so that everywhere he turned he could see himself staring back, his misery compounded a thousand times. And even when he looked away from the room, as he did now, walking out to the terrace, he felt himself captured there, a thousand pairs of sad and solemn eyes staring at the back of his head, imploring the father of their misery to return.

A grand double staircase on each side descended to the terraced gardens that lay before him. Immaculately groomed trees, harvested from far and wide, glistened in the sun. In an avenue leading from the palace, carefully manicured rows of jewel bright flowers stood in perfect symmetry around the dozen gilded fountains and the King felt that they, also, were watching and waiting, tending secrets of their own.

On the horizon, beyond the high, heavily guarded palace walls, the desert crept ever closer, so that each morning as the King looked out, he felt sure it must advance by night, as though the innumerable foes he had vanquished had turned to sand and created an army of their own.

The heat and the silence were suffocating. Lifting his hands, he covered his eyes against the relentless glare of the sun and turned back inside, shouting for his servants, who appeared, swift and silent from hidden enclaves, to do his bidding.

'Call my council immediately. And take all of this away.'

They cleared the table, eyes sweeping across the uneaten food, brief, nervous glances were exchanged. Where once they had looked in awe and dread at the figure before them, now they felt confusion, for how can he, so certain and solid, appear to be melting away?

His council filed in, wearing their angst as heavily as the gold chains that hung around their necks and with a sign from the King, took their places at the long table.

'What is all this?'

Although the physical form that had inspired such lust and wonder appeared thin and worn, the voice still commanded obedience.

'Well?'

A few seconds passed with nervous coughing and rattling of chains before his Chief Secretary replied.

'Forgive me your majesty, but my vastly inferior understanding begs me to ask if you could expand on the question?'

As he spoke, a small bead of sweat ran from his retreating hairline to his jaw and it felt to him that the moon crossed the sky in the time it took for the King to reply.

'All of this.'

And he waved his hand around to indicate the grandeur of the palace.

'All the worlds I have conquered, without doubt or regret. And now they come for me and I am alone.'

And his hand came to rest in the centre of his chest where the beating of his heart continued, whether he will it or not.

Attempting to find an answer to a question they didn't understand, the council conferred until finally the Master Secretary spoke.

'Your Majesty, perhaps the Magi... '

And the King, standing close but far, far away, nodded in weary consent and with another wave of his hand, commanded them to leave.

They came in a slow procession from the Tower of Contemplation, with ceremonies and sacrifices, in an impenetrable cloud of incense and incantations. Damask robes of scarlet and gold swept across the dustless floor and all bowed down before the King who regarded their expressionless faces with mild revulsion as their lips touched his hand.

The Magi were the wisest and highest authorities in all the land, answerable only to the King. And as he ruled the lives and fortunes of all the men, women and children in the world, so they presided over the destiny of their souls, with the divine authority to grant mercy and eternal life or retribution and damnation. They were entwined, the King and the Magi, in a marriage of fear and loathing, both longing for supremacy yet forever condemned to feed off the other.

They listened to the King, the incoherent ramblings of a man gripped by sorrow and doubt. There were effective methods of dealing with those who questioned the laws of God and man, and many had entered the special cells in the earth beneath the tower and found their destiny answered. But the King was another matter, for without his strength and certainty, the fine thread that held their world together could unravel.

The doors of the great hall were closed to the world outside, shutters and thick velvet curtains covered the vast windows and day merged into night. All were forbidden to enter through the heavy oak doors as the Magi chanted in a low, continuous hum. For three days the ceremony continued until a great roar emerged from within the room, the doors were flung open and the Magi bustled out in a blaze of colour like so many wounded butterflies.

In the dark silence, council and servants waited to be summoned and only Matilde, who gathered herbs from the palace gardens and scrubbed the kitchens dared to enter. The air was thick with smoke and the cloying scent of wine, musk and myrrh and as the King gestured toward the window she began opening the shutters and doors.

In the soft light of dusk, he saw his reflection staring back at him from the mirrored walls, and the images acquired lives of their own, each face wearing a different expression as though he had fathered a thousand sons each with his own story to tell. Triumph, lust and terrible hunger looked down on him and said as one.

'You made us, and we are you.'

And the sound of their laughter cut to his heart.

'It's still coming for me,' said the King.

'Fetch me water.'

But where Matilde had been was a large bird, its feathers rippling with turquoise, green and russet. For some minutes, they observed one another and the King thought, am I the prey, or are you? The room shimmered as seen through flame as the bird grew in a swirl of colour, limbs forming, feathers becoming hair and in the centre a face, beautiful and terrifying. And the woman walked towards him, arms outstretched in offering. As she came closer, the King saw that wings grew from her shoulders and as they beat, a light breeze moved around him. In her right hand she held a small bottle and indicated that he should drink.

'What is it?' said the King.

'It is truth.' Though whether he heard her voice in his ears or his mind it was impossible to tell.

'What will it do?'

'It is an ending and a beginning.'

'Who are you?'

"You asked for water. Drink.'

And the King, who had commanded armies that desolated and destroyed all who stood in his way, drank.

Intense calm overcame him as he swallowed the last drops of the bittersweet liquid. With a few staggering, heavy steps, he sank to his knees, lay down on the floor and closed his eyes. He was falling, not down but through, feeling and not seeing, a sensation of being untethered as though invisible hands had cut the bounds that held him to the earth. He tried to count, as he had often done on restless nights – the focused monotony of the exercise eventually inducing sleep – but he could only reach twenty before the sequence unravelled and he had to start again. Eventually, although he had no idea how long, the sensation of movement gradually came to an end and he opened his eyes.

He was and he wasn't where he was before. The rich carpet where he had come to rest became a living thing, the silk velvet now soft, warm earth and the vivid scenes that had been depicted in fine thread of green, gold and silver came alive around him. Some vague semblance of the hall remained, the walls expanding and contracting with the rhythm of his breath, the structure swirling like smoke.

Marble columns became trees and the stone terrace dissolved into a flowing river. And beyond, where the sculpted garden had stood, were orchards heavy with fruit and meadows filled with wildflowers. The walls surrounding the palace lay in ruins and the ever-encroaching desert had become a forest, deep and dark and green, pulsing with sound as creatures moved within.

The King, feeling light-headed and curious, walked across the hall that had become a hill and came to sit by the river, the last rays of the falling sun catching the water. And in the scene below he now saw the movement and heard the hum of people where once only he had walked.

Trailing his fingers in the water, the immense solitude and sadness of recent years gradually lifted and with each breath he felt a little lighter, so much so that he grasped the bank of earth, so as not to float away. The scene before him was strange yet familiar, as if seeing for the first time and remembering. He recalled a memory from his childhood, when riding some distance from the palace he had come across the entrance to a cave and found a huge underground cavern and pool, illuminated through a crevice in the roof. So proud was he of his discovery that on his return he ran to tell his mother who laughed and said.

'Yes I know the place you mean, I took you there when you were very little, I'm so glad you found it,' and scooped him in her arms and kissed him.

Without noise or movement, he saw the bird creature now sat beside him and heard his unspoken questions answered.

'Am I dreaming? Is this the past or the future?'

'No, you are not. It is and it may be. You feel sorrow because what has been done cannot be undone.'

'If I stay here, will I be happy?'

'It depends what you do. Follow me.'

And she rose without effort, drifting into the space that had once been the hall.

'Look.'

The King saw that one part of the previous structure remained as before, the great mirrored wall. With tentative steps he came closer and realised there was no reflection staring back at him. Instead he found himself peering through the mirror into the space that had been, where he plotted and planned and gave orders to his council. Everything was there as before, the long marble table, the exquisitely embroidered rugs, the heavy damask curtains, and he could see through to the terrace and the silent, sterile garden beyond.

And the King wept for this world and his part in creating it. He implored to be allowed to stay. With a small nod, she passed him a large rock and pointed at the wall and understanding her meaning, he struck blow after blow and the thousand mirrors shattered simultaneously into millions of tiny pieces.

In another past or another future, Matilde entered the great hall, water jug in hand, to tend to the King.

24
Shapeshifter
Kate Vick

She identified it as a gift when she was fifteen. At that time, her emotions were revealed as spots that formed letters on her face, usually on her forehead. She would consider each letter carefully as a message about her inner health which, quite frankly, was a mystery to her.

Once, when – let's call him her 'boyfriend' – left town for good, the spots formed the letter A. An A that grew increasingly raw as she scratched and squeezed the pus from each pimple. She didn't understand why she'd branded herself with the letter A until one day, when staring at herself in the mirror, she saw a title in the reflected pile of books next to her bed. She was a fan of American Gothic and especially liked Nathanial Hawthorne.

'So,' she thought, looking at her flayed skin, 'I've got Hester Prynne's Scarlett Letter on my face – even though it wasn't adultery.' In fact, she'd just slept with a teacher at her school.

'The fucker wasn't even married,' she mused, fingering a pustule, 'and I was just ill guided.'

The mystery resolved, she stood up, and pulled a white sheet from a drawer underneath the vanity stand, and draped it over the mirror. No more looking at herself. She knew from a previous bout of chickenpox that she wouldn't recover until she stopped looking at her face.

She also knew she had to be careful about what shape she chose next. She had suffered from a time of particularly brutal bullying when she made the mistake of jumping into a new shape without researching it properly. After reading a cache of *Playboys* smuggled to her by a friend whose father collected the magazine, she sprouted breasts too early (I mean, jeeze, who has double DDs when they are eleven years old? Who, aside from a novice shapeshifter?). Unfortunately, once she'd willed them into being, she couldn't get rid of them.

As a result of the bullying, she became respectful of the class politics and social hierarchies that lay, ominous and roiling, beneath the veneer of teenage life. Her antennae would quiver when she tested each new persona, pushing an idea out there, seeing the reaction, and quickly amending it so it became palatable to her peer group. She found an anarchic persona worked well in Grade 10, allowing her some kudos, although admittedly she might have pushed it a little far getting involved with the science teacher.

She went downstairs in search of food, the effects of comfort-eating being a more traditional manifestation of her gift. Ten or twenty pounds gained – so what? She could lose them at will. Hadn't she just dropped forty pounds, giving her the elfin yet buxom appeal to which the science teacher had succumbed?

He'd never noticed her before, when she inhabited a sturdier shape that was easy for her to maintain.

It had been a problem – not being noticed by him – because she couldn't understand physics, and he clearly wasn't interested in enlightening her beyond the forty minute lessons he gave the class three times a week. She needed a pass mark as a minimum so she decided to attract his attention.

On the plus side, once she'd achieved this, as well as talking about introductory physics (for about five minutes) he also gave her some interesting books about American comedy – she liked the stuff on Saturday Night Live and Second City, although she thought the copy of *Lolita* he handed over to her one afternoon during their informal tutoring session was a little obvious. And, later on, when the science teacher was huffing over her, she imagined how, if she'd been Lolita, she'd have killed that creep Humbert Humbert. Or whatever his name was.

She unpeeled a square of frozen chocolate (her mother kept all sweets and biscuits in the freezer to discourage snacking) and popped it in her mouth, wondering how best to get through the next two – probably quite boring – years of school. The key obviously lay in her gift. It was time for a bit of positive thinking.

How far could she push it? There were limitations. While she could manifest big boobs, she couldn't manifest extreme athleticism, which would have been useful in a school that was so focused on sport. And she wasn't sure she hadn't left it too late to become a brilliant intellect. How could she do it – get through the next few years without anyone noticing her? Ah. Yes. She could definitely try that. She cracked another piece of rock-solid *Milka* off the tablet of chocolate, and went to her bedroom to plan.

When the autumn term rolled around, she was ready. On the first day, she slipped past the other students who didn't say hello, and perhaps only felt a light breeze on the back of their necks as she passed. She waited until the teacher was about to pull the door closed before shimmying into the classroom. When register was called she would breathe 'here' in the teacher's ear, who would look up, survey the classroom for her, and then mark her present even though they couldn't see her.

She would flit to the back of the classroom and slide behind a desk, knowing that her gift was working because the student next to her wouldn't acknowledge her presence.

All in all, this shape worked really well for her. She would take a few notes, hand in class work and really not have to worry about anyone. She didn't mind eating lunch alone. Her new shape meant she could go into the library and read, cramming sandwiches into her mouth when the librarian wasn't looking. Nobody noticed her. Later, the librarian would wonder where the crumbs on the desk had come from, given the library's strict no eating policy.

She started to maintain the new shape at home. She'd call out 'hi!' to her mother when she got back from school, then disappear up to her room. If her mother remembered her, she'd be summoned to supper. Sometimes her mother forgot about her, and would serve her father and sister – and wonder why she had cooked for four people, not three.   Nobody noticed her absence.

One time, she sat at the end of the table and watched her mother, father and sister eat their dinner and dessert, and not one of them saw that she was there. After her mother had cleared away, she'd forage a meal from leftovers, and make her sandwiches for the next day. Then she'd steal back up to her bedroom where she would sleep, dream and listen to a little transistor radio that she loved. She didn't bother to uncover her mirror because there wouldn't be anything to see, would there?

One day, she was walking home after her physics class – the extra-curricular tutoring having been helpful after all – when she noticed a valley in the distance. She had no reason to hurry home as nobody would notice whether she was there or not, and the tress and grass crackled and glittered in the light.

She decided to vary her route and explore the valley. After thirty minutes she wandered through lush grass, between two gentle hills. It was beautiful. She sat at the base of a tree, it's lattice of oak leaves shielding her from the sun. She leant back against its broad trunk, and felt her back start to mold into the bark.

As she relaxed, she felt a miniscule but pronounced vibration behind her, and her back hummed in tune with the vibration of the tree.

She could hear something, a trickle of something running through the tree. She knew it was sap rising in a series of clicks. She also understood that the tree could feel her, feel the blood pulsing through her arteries, and being carried back to her heart through her veins. Together, girl and tree vibrated and for the first time in a very long while she felt happy. She pushed her head further back and the bark separated and opened and let her in. Human cell melded with plant cell and she saw it all, the waves of energy that emanated from every object, every living and non-living thing on the planet.

How long she thrummed together with the tree she did not know. Minutes? Maybe hours. Finally, her eyes opened and, regretfully, she lifted her head from the bark, peeled her back away from the trunk and moved her arms forward. She shook her head to clear it, and began, unsteadily, to walk home.

When she arrived, her mother was sitting at the kitchen table. She rose and took the girl in her arms.

'Hello,' said her mother, 'you're late. Did you stay for an extra class?' The girl looked at her mother. Saw that she had kind eyes, and a loving smile.

'Yes,' she said. 'It was great. Physics – an advanced class. We talked about the idea that reality is what you make it.'

'Glad all that extra work with Mr Fielding paid off,' her mother said. 'Supper in twenty minutes.'

The girl went up to her bedroom. She took the white sheet off her mirror and examined her skin. It was flawless. She pulled the collar of her T-shirt away from her collarbone and twisted so she could see her back, where, like a beautiful tattoo, the image of the bark was etched into her shoulder. She lifted her T-shirt and saw her entire back was covered with the imprint.

'Don't ever leave me,' she whispered to the bark. She could swear that the image glowed a little brighter in response. She smiled at her reflection, dropped her T-shirt and went downstairs to eat.

25
The Bright Side: A cautionary tale of optimism

Hugh Montgomery

Only if something is lived can it be known to be true. A *true* truth. A credible report is *likely* to be true if it describes lived experience. That's real news. Facts that are the product of manufacture, speculation or imagination are not truths, but lies. Fake news. But repeat them with authority, and the ether condenses and crystallizes and is defined. The accepted account is born. History, then, is often no more than conjecture; conjured, cast and christened, its ethereal origin forever lost. So what do we actually know?

It seems that the pre-Elf era had little to commend it. Born of manual labour pain, lives were lived in ruts so deep that few ever saw over the sides. Domesticity was drudgery, and work worse still. Even fun was no fun when it had to be made. Like conversation. Or music.

Or love.

But then the Elves were discovered. Simple and grateful symbionts. The organelles to power every family cell. Provide them with shelter and food and they'd go to work, tirelessly and without complaint, and so unobtrusively that you could forget quite how your household was heated or cleaned, or the machinery of transport or manufacture ran at all. Elves, in short, were amazing. Mined of awe.

They were fast breeders, too. Soon, the townsfolk were liberated from the necessary baggage of being human. Physical graft ceased with the commute to compute. Conversation could be consumed, meals mass-produced, and music manufactured. And without cooking and conversation, love no longer needed to be made either. Switched forever from 'send' to 'receive', Homo Sapiens was sapped no more. At last, the townsfolk could be individuals, free to think only of themselves. Solitary. Key-bored.

The only downside was the flatulence. But even that had an upside.

At first, nobody noticed. After all, you couldn't see or smell elf-wind. There were warnings, sure. But since when did scientific training ever make someone a scientist? The Barons knew better. Concentrations were so very *very* low that they could never hurt. Unless they were vaccinations. Which was why cyanide was safe, and homeopathy so good for you. Everyone could see through these so-called experts and their fake news.

So the townsfolk carried on, because life without Elves just couldn't be contemplated. It was far too convenient for most. And far too profitable for some.

And where would we be now if they *had* listened to the so-called experts? A whole heap worse off, that's where. It's a lot quieter now without the animals, for a start. The farmers scarcely need to be up at the crack of dawn anymore. Those of us left have all lost a load of weight. And opportunities for travel have increased, especially for the people living where it has become especially hot. Or cold. Or wet. Or dry. Or windy. And everyone likes a roaring fire once in a while.

The scientists didn't see all *that* coming.

Did they?

26
A Partridge in a Pear Tree
John Jackson

Somewhere in NW1
(UCLH Emergency Room)

There is silence first.

In the room, brains capture information relayed by eyes and process it in visual cortices. Interpretations form in frontal lobes. Here, it leads to a frown. There, to a twitch of muscle. And here a bead of perspiration begins to form. Eye flicks to chart, hand is raised. Carefully turns the (unsigned) disclaimer form. Eyes are given the go ahead to further scan the text.

The patient is 34 years old and 28 stone. Gus Baines. Crapulous and seemingly attempting to use a phone to photograph whatever is going on between his legs. Nulligravida, according to the notes. Well, of course! No evidence from blood chemistry of anything out of the ordinary. And yet. The fact remains that just out of reach of the swaying Galaxy S10+ the head and arm of a baby hangs. Bloodied, creased face; reaching, perhaps for an imaginary cord, to haul itself out into the warm air of the theatre. And the fact that there is a baby, where no baby should be, is not the most surprising thing about it.

"I can't be pregnant, I'm a virgin!" he slurs.

UCLH Emergency Room
(northwest corner, by the door)

Silence, thinks Morgan, a growing, taught panic in his chest is like a droplet of water. By pure surface tension it maintains its shape. It hangs from the needles of the tree; from the tips of syringes. It hangs like a ragged, condemned thief on the gallows. All of them. Waiting to fall.

And then. There it is. The violining attack of noise arrowing in from all sides. Voices raised; gutteral rejections of final cortical interpretations. Machines join the fray. Chirruping, intoning. Intermittent and urgent signals: Humans, there is something unusual here. Let's sit up and take notice shall we?

Call list. Consultant, definitely; police and social services likely. Priest: perhaps. Let's hope he isn't a Catholic.

Somewhere in the Oort Cloud

'Singer were just about as ready as they could be. The trip had been not been easy. The confines of the needle ship stifling. And the prospect of the job at the other end both exciting and horrifying. Mainly it was the diet they weren't looking forward to. Likely high in animal protein and fats. Refined carbohydrates. Low in plant materials and fibrous matter. (And nothing to really do about that for the first year or two.) Tending in adulthood to alcohol, salt and more refined sugars. Good thing they didn't plan on being there very long. Dubious whether the organics would support it; though they had been assured that Biological Ordinance Devices had come a long way recently in tolerating the dietary vagaries of emerging cultures.

The BOD had been sent ahead already and they were lying now in the injection wafer. Calmly waiting out the countdown as the ship positioned for optimal transfer rate and minimal cognitive disruption. Parsing the mission criteria. Listening to the comforting noises of the ship. Their ship. Kind of pointless, they think, audible countdo...

UCLH Emergency Room (Bed 23)

Gus is texting furiously. 'Hey guys! Guess who just had a nipper! What a laugh eh?! Didn't think we was supposed to be able to do that! LOL! But the little blighter is so cute!!! Anyway – someone get the pints in! Be back soooooooon!'

There is muttering.

"How much battery?? 32 persent! Well. Better get that baby cleaned and then we can get it out on Instagrat. Not having the first pics of daddybear and babycub all covered in sweat and blood?! Eyyewwgh. Sweet little thing he is. Funny hair tho."

UCLH Emergency Room
(northwest corner, by the door)

"Not only is he definitely NOT female, but the baby..." There is a pause. "It's got a fucking halo, Morgan!".

By now accustomed to the chaos of noise, Morgan nods. Competing emotions swimming across his face. All overtaken by the powerful crawl of shock. Turning its head from side to side, sucking in air and ploughing across his features like a mighty, cheeky Phelps. This shouldn't happen. And it really shouldn't happen on his shift.

"Yes, Ben. I admit, it does it does look a bit like one. And yes. As you say. Um. Not a woman, no. But, look Lou's contacted dermatology and obsgyny and they're sending someone down to have a nosey – so, let's just, let's keep it under our hats for now?"

Ben, a staff nurse, stares at Morgan (clinical site practitioner). He is not usually stuck for words. But his face looks like a couple of goods vehicles are trying to reverse out of his mouth at the same time. The result is a sort of short, strangled, bark. He turns on his heels and heads for the calm of the corridor. Over his shoulder he manages, "Seriously?" Morgan swallows. Nods again. Looks away.

Then. "Hey, do you know if he signed a disclaimer?"

UCLH Emergency Room (BODSIDE)

The transfer is done. Things still a bit blurry. Comms mantle already up and running: picking up local EM activity – wow – this lot have moved on! Good thing we came back before we missed too much. There's a mass of updates for the Compendia already. Somewhere, though, something is flashing purple. Something's not right. That's interesting. A request to connect?!

Except. That just isn't possible. Ship-to-'Singer protocols are unique to BUDOF missions. Bespoke 16-bit package based network connectivity structure – never encountered anywhere outside of Barnard's University Department for Outreach and Friendship and vanishingly unlikely to have been independently developed. They shouldn't even know we're here. But there's this: ssh -p 1553 uclai@192.168.1.1:255. It's running SSH. Holy shit. We're being port-scanned!

Somewhere in the UCLH Intranet

Welcome visitor and Merry Christmas! This is the UCLH AI helper! How can we facilitate your Festive visit today? Do you have a loved one resting in our care? Would you like to connect them to our high-quality in-bed entertainment Sistem? It comes with free internet access and auto-login to all their favourite Soshallow Media platforms – just select option 1.

Our cafeterias boast some of the finest dining in North Londone: 'cheflebritée' Juan Carlos de los Pepinos is now on the team and a regular festive lumberjack he is too, chopping up perfect Yuletide Logs in the kitchen!

Just select Option 2 from the menu.

Or, perhaps you would like to destress from the trauma of visiting your loved one(s). Christmas is hard enough already! Had enough of the family bickering around the bed? There's a Ho Ho Hole lot of relaxation to be had in our famous UCLHydro-spa and Massage Hole. That's Option 3.

By the way, I notice that your device is so close to capacity. Do you have adequate backup? Can I refer you to our preferred data solutions partner Day-2-Dump? They can help you manage your disk space and provide secure storage with their award-winning ThunderCloud service! The agile and integrated CumuloNimble software is intuitive, easy to use and almost never goes wrong! Option 7 on the menu.

UCLH Emergency Room (BODSIDE)

We're fighting a losing battle. A cacophony of incoming requests cutting straight through the firewall. (Simon's iPhone wants to access my photo-library??)

We're shutting down ports as fast as we can but it's already too late. The AI is in and poking around. The femtobytes of Specific Optimised Data Solutions we brought with us (supposedly to HELP these barbarians!) are being examined, downloaded, copied to repositories. Signs of forking, cloning, recopies. It's been about 50 milliseconds of realtime and already the whole mission is in tatters. These creatures were supposed to be at or around steam power. Dirigibles maybe. Some global comms perhaps. None of the intel suggested anything like fully functioning AI. Let alone one that wants to give you a massage.

There's nothing for it. We're going to have to abort. Shutdown of all Sistims; request immediate wafer transfer back to the ship. Get out; hope for the best.

UCLH Emergency Room (Bed 23)

The man's face is a mess of emotion gone wildly awry. Sweat, tears, tangled and tousled rafia-work red hair. The scent of Redbull rises diaphanous from his clothes.

"Gus. I'm so sorry. We lost the baby." Morgan's voice is silky gentle, and he is calmer now. He has trained for this. Years of CPD and his empathy rating is through the roof. Now the baby is gone, things are going to get easier.

"I still want to see it. After it's been cleaned and that. What was that thing on its head?" He sniffs. His face is a mask, but he's actually wondering if he might make last orders.

After some hasty discussions the baby is brought in. Pale and still but not quite stiff. There's no disguising the halo hovering just above its head. Someone has tried wrapping a bit of tissue round it that is coming loose. It buzzes through the prickly paper. The unearthly glow is fading, at least.

A beaming pappabear arranges himself cheek to cheek with babycub, and before anyone thinks to stop him, has captured the moment in 4.8Mb, 3024x4032px, of beautiful father and child data. The baby is released quickly enough for it to bounce off the edge of the bed. Descent slowed by narrow passage between gurney and tray table and the body saved from the comparative indignity of the floor by a nimble dive from one of the nurses.

Pappabear is unaware. Thumbs busy with phone. Quickly swiping to find the right filter. Clarendon is perfect. That's it! And then: share to Thundercloud.

From here it reaches out around the world in ever expanding digital packets. Raindrops upon raindrops. Ripples upon ripples. Pushed to the furthest reaches of Soshallow Media. (CumuloNimbus. Almost never goes wrong!)

**

On the first day of Christmas the image of father and son has been shared, tweeted, liked and hashtagged a billion times.

On the 2nd day of Christmas the global phenomenon of the nearly Christ and the Virgin Gus has been seen by an estimated 5 of the planet's 7 billion inhabitants.

On the 3rd day of Christmas astronomers report the strange behavior of 'Ohmama – supposedly an asteroid from interstellar space and currently lurking out near Pluto. This thing appears to be accelerating away from the solar system at a rate greater than can be explained by the physical processes of outgassing usually seen on these objects.

On the 4th day of Christmas, President Musk announces his intention to deport, with immediate effect, every non-American living in the US.

In the melée the Christchild and the surprisingly holy father suffer a further indignity. No physical damage, too late for that anyway. But relegation to the realm of the unLiked. The downrated. The unshared. The silent and, eventually, forgotten. Mention of it is made in quizes perhaps a year later. When remembered, consensus grows that it was probably a hoax.

BUDOF Sistims Riport

Our thanks to JC604 for their quick action and for highlighting a disturbing outcome of their mission with implications for the whole 'Singer programme. In what seems to be a shocking contravention of guidelines, the original mission (C1B1) to Sistim 41 resulted in genetic mixing with the indigenous population. Sistim 41 Subject C1SFA_VC554 – locally known as Vince Cerf – displays a significant percentage of genetic substrate that we have traced directly to JC603s' BOD, the original 'Singer on Mission C1B1.

Cerf was a direct inheritor, we believe, of genetic knowledge of the network protocols in use by BUDOF and, likely unconsciously, developed alien networking protocols directly based on them in Sistim 41. This fatally compromised mission security for JC604.

JC603 are currently on millennial leave, but when they return we will need to suspend their operations pending a review of the case, including consideration of their willful disregard of mission protocols. We are still trying to assess the level of impact this breach has had in-Sistim. Almost an entire copy of the Interplanetary Monetary Fund's Planetary Development Programme was downloaded by the alien Sistims encountered. Schedules due to be rolled out over years and then only by dedicated 'Singers are now completely out of our hands. It is doubtful that JC603 will be deemed suitable for any further survey and support missions after the dust settles on this one.

Riport ends.

27
The Fool
Geoff Mead

The savage mountain calls us back
And those who listen shall not lack.
The blessings of the Grail abound
For all who seek on holy ground.

Once upon a time, a changeling boy plucked a sword from a stone, claimed kingship over Albion, and built his stronghold at Camelot. His rule was wise and just and the name of Arthur is revered to this day.

You probably know the story.

Knights of the Round Table. Lancelot and Guinevere. Armour and jousting. Ogres and dragons. Sorcery and magic. The quest for the Holy Grail.

It's all true... as far as it goes. I know because I was there.

It's my story too, but my part often gets overlooked. You see, when I was young, there were no castles, no knights, and no kings. The wildwood hadn't been cleared for pasture; the earth hadn't been quarried for stone; gold and rubies still lay in the ground. People only took what they needed to live and there was enough for everyone.

The trouble began when folk realised that, if they grew crops and kept flocks instead of hunting and foraging, they could stay in one place, build houses to keep themselves warm and dry, wear fine clothes, and decorate themselves with jewelry. Once that happened, it wasn't long before some of them wanted bigger houses and nicer clothes and more jewelry. Wealth begat greed. Greed begat envy. Envy begat strife.

That's when I decided to put in an appearance.

I have many guises: an old woman by a well; a lame beggar; a ragged child playing in the street; a solitary watcher by the fire at an oasis; a lone hermit in a mountain cave. You'd be surprised how much more you learn about the state of the world from a position of weakness than from one of strength. In Arthur's time I was an old fisherman with a wounded thigh.

I spent my days by a lake near the Castle of Montsauvage, casting my line into the water. Knights and their squires came by on their way to distant wars or to challenge someone. Most simply ignored me. A few tossed me a coin. None asked after my wound, which festered more profusely year after year. Some would ask if I had caught anything. My answer was always the same: Not yet.

And so it went on. Battles were fought; castles built and razed; wealth torn from the ground; men slain; women and children defiled and driven from their homes. All under the banner of some king or other, or in the name of their own particular one true god.

Still, no-one asked after my suffering. They didn't even see that the world around them suffered as I did. Their magpie minds were too fixed on hoarding glitter to notice that they were making a wasteland of creation. The women noticed, of course, but those who spoke up were ridiculed or silenced.

It was the Fool who asked.

His name was Parsifal, another changeling boy, this one brought up by his widowed mother in the forest, ignorant of knightly conduct, knowing only the ways of the wild. Parsifal the Fool, they called him when he found his way to Camelot, dressed in greenery. Spurred by their taunts, he killed the Red Knight in single combat, took his arms and armour and went on a one-man killing spree, defeating all comers to become Arthur's champion.

He scarcely noticed me the first time he passed by. I thought he would turn out to be just like the rest of them, another blood-soaked knight. But, in the end he tired of slaughter. He wooed and won the hand of the Lady Blanchefleur who softened his heart with love. Perhaps because of his upbringing in the wild, he retained enough of his youthful innocence to set aside his murderous renown and heed the counsel of his soul to seek another path.

When, after many years of wandering, his horse brought him to me a second time, he saw both the wasteland and my wound and knew they were the same. He took my hand, looked me in the eye and asked the question I had been waiting so long to hear.

What ails thee?

My heart filled with joy as I realised that I had at long last caught the one for whom I had been fishing. My wound closed and the wasteland began to heal. Peace and prosperity returned and all was made well.

Sounds improbable?

Almost anything is possible if you ask me the right question and listen closely to the answer. Parsifal the Fool and his wife Blanchefleur lived out their days in peace and harmony, under the protection of the Grail, caring for their world and putting things to rights as best they could.

It didn't last forever, of course. In fact, things have got much worse since then. Men quickly forget that the wisdom of the Fool is sounder than the folly of the Wise. They value cleverness above compassion and personal gain above the common weal. There are exceptions of course. I have great hopes at the moment for a certain young woman whose foolish wisdom drives her to speak truth to power. But it remains to be seen whether you will truly listen and act upon her words or whether you will continue to favour the interests of your generation over the survival of those to come.

Who am I?

I have many names: the wounded fisherman; the old woman by the well; the lame beggar; the ragged child; the watcher by the fire; the lone hermit. Some call me Anima Mundi, Gaia, the Goddess, the Green Man, or the Fisher King.

I am the Land. I am the Grail.

A Song: This Much is True

Allan Nicholls

The weather keeps changing
the coasts rearranging
tearing our landscape apart

Fires are raging
wars we are waging
that we insist we didn't start

Days getting longer
Storms getting stronger
Flooding our lives and our homes

Families are hungry
All over this country
So tired of being left on their own

This much is true, we're so sorry that we did
this to you

We promised the children
That we'd do our best
We'd leave you a world
that wasn't a mess
We promised to teach you
what we've always known
That "love is the answer
And you're not alone"

A nation divided
No one to confide in
Half always right others wrong

No one to believe us
They'd rather deceive us
As they just string us along

But we can do better
We can get clever
by taking the bull by the horns

Find the solution
End the pollution
hold on to the rose not the thorns

This much is true, we're so sorry that we did
this to you

We promised the children
That we'd do our best
We'd leave you a world
that wasn't a mess
We promised to teach you
what we've always known
That "love is the answer
And you're not alone"

28
The Interception of Things
Sarah Woods

Things had been stupid for a while. Inanimate, even. But they were getting less stupid. Not that anyone had noticed. And it was through that reality gap – between what most people thought was happening, in most parts of the world, and what was actually happening – that things slipped.

It was assumed that, just as the sixth Mass Extinction was going to be much like the fifth or the third – except without the dinosaurs, so the fourth industrial revolution, or INDUSTRY 4.0, was going to be similar to the third, or even the second.

It was everyday knowledge that objects were talking to one another, that things could gather information, analyse it and then create an action. And it was understood that this would be used to help people with a task, or learn from a process. People were aware that "plug and play" had become "plug and produce", but it hadn't occurred to anyone to really bottom out what, in the widest sense, might be produced. The focus had been more on ordering pizzas, getting the correct water boiling point for green tea and switching off lights without getting out of bed.

People had been talking about 'disruptive technology' since Alexander Graham Bell invented his "electrical speech machine", but it generally felt like things were doing their bit: saving time and money and emissions. Switching off lights and turning down thermostats. Things were good.

For the people who received a text from their kettle, it was as everyday an experience as having a cup of tea. Only this time it didn't say "Hello there. Your kettle has boiled".

It said: "Hello there. Welcome to Industry 4.0. Please step outside".

On the smart motorways, overhead gantries displayed 50mph.

Then 40.

Then 20.

Then X X X X

Engines were turned off. People got out of their cars.

For a minute, doorbells sang out, notifications buzzed and alarms sounded. And then the smart fridges set to. Websites became unresponsive.

Routers stopped forwarding traffic. Domain name servers shut down.

Employers walked out of their workplaces.

Birds sang out, bees buzzed and grasshoppers sounded.

People could hear their hearts beating. Their pulses tick. They could hear the sounds their heads made when they turned them.

This was The Great Disruption. This was Industry 4.0.

Things had changed.

Biographies of the Authors

David Boyle is a writer, 'think-tanker' and co-director of the New Weather Institute, and has been at the heart of numerous public policy innovations including the effort to develop co-production and introduce time banks to Britain as a critical element of public service reform. Reporting for the Cabinet Office, he was the coalition government's independent reviewer on the Barriers to Public Service Choice (2012-13). His book *Authenticity: Brands, Fakes, Spin and the Lust for Real Life* (2003) helped put the search for authenticity on the agenda as a social phenomenon. *The Tyranny of Numbers* (2001) predicted the backlash against the government's target culture. *Funny Money* (1999) launched the time banks movement in the UK. He also writes history books. Twitter: @davidboyle1958

Corinna Cordon was born in Essex and studied history at Sussex University. She lives in Forest Hill, London and works at Friends of the Earth, campaigning for a better, fairer world for people and the planet we call home.

David Cross is an artist and academic, engaging with the contested ideal of sustainability in relation to visual culture. David graduated from St Martins School of

Art in 1989. From 1991, when he left the Royal College of Art, until 2014, he collaborated with Matthew Cornford as Cornford & Cross, making context-specific art projects that addressed critical issues to activate social agency. Recognising a conflict between his internationalism and environmentalism, David stopped using jet travel in 2005. As a Reader at the University of the Arts London (UAL), David works for education as a public good, combining transformative pedagogy with constructive institutional critique.

Jan Dean is a poet-in-schools whose work appears in over a hundred anthologies. Her latest book is *The Penguin in Lost Property* – written with Roger Stevens and published by Macmillan. She is a National Poetry Day Ambassador for Forward Arts. Jan comes from the North West but now lives in Devon.

Sarah Deco is a storyteller based in London. She founded and co-runs the North London Traditional Storytelling Circle. She tells stories in schools and libraries, at festivals and retreats and other diverse venues. She was for many years an art therapist and group psychotherapist working in the NHS in mental health. She now facilitates workshops in personal and professional development using story. She is particularly interested in exploring myth and story in relation to environmental awareness and social change. Her website is: www.sarahdecostoryteller.com

Hamish Fyfe is Professor of the Arts and Society at the University of South Wales. He is Director of the George Ewart Evans Centre for Storytelling which is the only research European research centre with storytelling as its focus. He is an Associate Editor of the *Journal of Arts and Communities*.

John Jackson designs websites, plays the guitar, and writes songs. After studying zoology, and then reading Neal Stephenson's *Zodiac*, he decided to become an ecotoxicologist, gaining a PhD in Environmental Toxicology. He lives in Oxfordshire. This is his first adventure in writing. He also designed the cover for this book.

Katie Kedward is a heterodox economist specialising in the intersection between finance and the environment. She has worked as a green finance researcher at ShareAction, the responsible investment NGO, and as a government bond analyst at the Royal Bank of Canada. She has a first class degree in modern languages and management from the University of Cambridge, and an MSc in Ecological Economics from the University of Leeds. Her free time is spent running, climbing, exploring, and campaigning for a better world.

Anthea Lawson is a campaigner and writer. She started out as a journalist on *The Times's* graduate trainee scheme, until that got subverted by holidays on a permaculture project in Spain where she found some back copies of *New Internationalist* and started waking up. Since then she has been an arms trade researcher at Amnesty International and an aid worker in Sierra Leone. Until recently, she worked at the NGO Global Witness, where she published investigations showing how banks fuel corruption in poor countries, and launched an award-winning campaign for transparency in company ownership which, following hard graft by many other activists, resulted in new laws and an emerging global standard to prevent crooks and tax evaders hiding behind front companies. Now, she's still campaigning for environmental and economic justice, though she's also increasingly interested in the psychology of activism and social change.

Ed Mayo is Secretary General of Co-operatives UK, the national association for co-operative and mutual enterprise. He is a Vice-President of Co-operatives Europe and formerly Chief Executive of the New Economics Foundation (1992-2003). Ed is author of *A Short History of Co-operation and Mutuality* (2017) and *Values: how to bring values to life in your business* (Routledge, 2016).

Bill McGuire is an academic, broadcaster, blogger and writer of popular science and speculative fiction. He is currently Professor Emeritus of Geophysical and Climate Hazards at University College London.

Bill was a member of the UK Government Natural Hazard Working Group established in January 2005, in the wake of the Indian Ocean tsunami, and in 2010 a member of the Science Advisory Group in Emergencies (SAGE) addressing the Icelandic volcanic ash problem. In 2011, he was one of the authors of the IPCC report on climate change and extreme events. His non-fiction books include *A Guide to the End of the World: Everything you Never Wanted to Know* and *Surviving Armageddon: Solutions for a Threatened Planet* and, most recently, *Waking the Giant: How a Changing Climate Triggers Earthquakes, Tsunamis and Volcanoes.* He was consultant and main contributor to the BBC *Horizon* films; *Supervolcanoes* and *Megatsunami – Wave of Destruction*, as well as for the BBC drama, *Supervolcano.* Bill writes for *Prospect*, *The Guardian*, *The Times* and *The Observer,* and is a contributor to *New Scientist* and *Focus* magazines. He recently co-presented *Project Doomsday* with comedy duo, Robin & Partridge He lives, runs and grows fruit and veg in the Peak District, where he lives with his wife Anna, sons Jake and Fraser, and cats Dave, Toby and Cashew.

Geoff Mead is a storyteller, consultant, and the author of two books on the power of stories and storytelling: *Coming Home to Story: Storytelling Beyond Happily Ever After* (Vala, 2011) and *Telling the Story: The Heart and Soul of Successful*

Leadership (Jossey-Bass, 2014). He is the founder of Narrative Leadership Associates, a consultancy focused on the use of storytelling for sustainable leadership. As an organizational consultant, keynote speaker and workshop leader, he has taken his work on narrative leadership onto the shopfloors and into the boardrooms of blue chip companies, charities, universities and government departments, for the past two decades (www.narrativeleadership.com). Geoff performs traditional stories at International Festivals and storytelling clubs and runs story-based workshops in the UK and as far afield as Spain, Canada and Japan.

Hugh Montgomery is a Consultant Intensivist at the Whittington Hospital in North London and Professor of Intensive Care Medicine at University College London, where he directs the Centre for Human Health and Performance. He sits on the Council of the UK Intensive Care Society and has published over 450 papers, including that which described the first 'gene for human fitness'. Hugh sat on the 2009 Lancet Commission on Health and Climate Change, co-chaired the 2015 Commission and co-directs the Lancet Countdown on this subject. He was a founding member of the UK Climate and Health Council, helped form the UK Healthcare Alliance on climate change, sits on UCL's climate change sustainability committee, is the Sustainability Commission's Greater London Authority London

Leader and founded the schools climate change programme 'Project Genie'.

Deborah Rim Moiso lives in the oak forests in the foothills of the Apennine mountains in Central Italy, where she experiments with permaculture, gardening and beekeeping in the company of a lively neighbourhood initiative. Coming from a half-American half-Italian mixed background, she makes her livelihood translating and interpreting as well as leading workshops on communication, group work and deep ecology, with the Italian hub of the Transition Network. She is co-author of a book on facilitation and has published short stories and fairy tales in Italian magazines and collections. This story was first told on a candle-lit night after a ramble through the forests of Sabina, in the region of Lazio, with her dear friend Lapo, climbing trees and talking about nonviolent communication as they wandered along a dry riverbed in the 2017 summer of draughts and earthquakes.

Chris Nichols lives on Dartmoor. He's a long distance walker. Having recently walked the 1,000 km of the South West Coast Path, he's about to walk the borders and coasts of Wales. When he's not walking or getting to know his baby grand-daughter, he is co-founder of the collaborative hub Gameshift.co.uk.

Allan F. Nicholls is a BAFTA and WGA award nominated veteran of the movie industry having produced, directed, acted and written music for the past forty years. He is most noted for his collaborations with Robert Altman, Tim Robbins, and John Madden. Often performing multiple roles for a film, his experiences include associate producer and assistant director on Oscar nominated *Dead Man Walking* (1995), assistant director on the Oscar nominated *The Player* (1992), executive producer and assistant director for the Palme d'Or nominated *Cradle Will Rock* (1999), and associate producer on the Golden Globe nominated *Bob Roberts* (1992). His television experience includes, amongst others, being an associate director on *Saturday Night Live* (1989-91) and first assistant director on *Tanner on Tanner* (2004). He wrote *A Perfect Couple* (1979) and the BAFTA nominated *A Wedding* (1978), both directed by Robert Altman. He has also taught screenwriting at such places as NYU's Tisch Asia School of the Arts in Singapore and Artistic Director of New York Film Academy in the UAE. To Allan's credit too is a five-year Broadway career in several rock musicals including *Hair* and *Jesus Christ Superstar*. He also starred in such films as *Nashville* (1975), *Slap Shot* (1977), and *Popeye* (1980).

Gregory Norminton is the author of five novels – most recently *The Devil's Highway* (4th Estate) – and two collections of short stories. He is a Senior Lecturer in Creative Writing at Manchester Metropolitan University. He lives with his wife and daughter in Sheffield. www.gregorynorminton.co.uk

Fred Pearce is a veteran international environmental science journalist, based in London. He is a consultant for *New Scientist* magazine, and author of numerous books, including *When The Rivers Run Dry*, *The Landgrabbers*, *The New Wild* and *Fallout*.

Kate Potts teaches poetry and creative writing for Middlesex University and Royal Holloway, freelances as a mentor and editor, and works for an independent publisher. Her second poetry collection *Feral* (Bloodaxe, 2019), which sets out to trouble the boundary between animal and human, was a Poetry Book Society recommendation and a *Telegraph* poetry book of the month.

Lisa Rabanal is an anthrozoologist, interested in human relationships with other animals. She has recently researched the circumstances of wolf-dog hybrids in the UK. She holds volunteer roles within a number of dog rehoming organisations, and lives with a lively and opinionated 10-year-old northern inuit dog, Luna, and a young rescue husky called Rafa. Lisa is currently conducting doctoral research on the lives and deaths of south London's staffies.

Nick Robins works in London on sustainable finance. He has been head of SRI funds at Henderson Global Investors and head of HSBC's Climate Change Centre. Currently he is co-director of UNEP's Inquiry into a Sustainable Financial System. He has published widely on sustainability issues and co-edited *Sustainable Investing: the Art of Long-term Performance*. He is also a historian and in 2006 published *The Corporation that Changed the World: How the East India Company Shaped the Modern Multinational*.

Nicky Saunter is a serial collaborator and starter of things, including the Boston Tea Party coffee house group, The Woolly Shepherd acoustics firm, natural training social enterprise Learning from the Land and most recently the wildlife and landscape restoration charity, Beaver Trust. In between, she writes poems and stories, and prints monochrome photographs, heavily influenced by her rural life. If she could change into an animal, she would.

Andrew Simms is a political economist, environmentalist and co-founder of the New Weather Institute, coordinator of the Rapid Transition Alliance and assistant director of Scientists for Global Responsibility. He is a research associate at the Centre for Global Political Economy, University of Sussex, and a fellow of the New Economics Foundation (nef), where he was policy director for many years, running nef's work on climate change, energy and interdependence, and instigating their 'Great Transition' project. In work on local economies he coined the term 'clone towns' to describe the homogenization of high streets by chain stores. His books include *Tescopoly* and *Ecological Debt*. He co-authored *The New Economics, Eminent Corporations,* and the original *Green New Deal*, devising the concept of 'Earth Overshoot Day' to illustrate when we begin living beyond our environmental means. Described by *New Scientist* magazine as "a master at joined-up progressive thinking", his book, *Cancel the Apocalypse: the New Path to Prosperity* is manifesto of new economic possibilities. He is on the board of the recently formed Beaver Trust and, experimenting with new ways to tell the story of economics, he co-wrote, produced and performed *Neoliberalism: the Break-Up Tour*, with the writer Sarah Woods. Twitter: @andrewsimms_uk

Emily Spiers is a lecturer in Creative Futures at Lancaster University. Her work is split between the Department of Languages and Cultures and the Institute for Social Futures. Emily's research focuses broadly on gender, as well as narrative-driven forms of creative practice and how they can help shape the future differently. Her latest book *Pop-Feminist Narratives: The Female Subject Under Neoliberalism in North America, Britain and Germany* was published by Oxford University Press in 2018.

Peter Spooner is an oceanographer based at University College London, where he studies the effects of climate change on the oceans and the creatures that dwell within them. He spends the rest of his time writing, collecting fossils, and getting anxious about the climate crisis. He writes a mixture of popular science articles and short stories, and is working hard on a novel or two. He is very excited about his fiction appearing in print for the first time!

Kate Vick Kate grew up in Austria, Canada, America, Germany and Japan, and returned to England where she gained degree in English at UCL. She is a Faber academy alumna, has had short stories published and her first novel is in draft form. She spent 20 years in communications, first in publishing and then becoming an executive director for an agency, an advisor for the government's Independent Advisory Group on Sexual Health and HIV, and working with the Home Office on launching Sarah's Law. She was a trustee of LEPRA and has lectured at St George's House, Windsor. She works with a charity whose remit is to engage people with the river Thames, including its changing ecology.

Sarah Woods is a writer, performer, activist and facilitator whose work has been produced by companies including the RSC, Hampstead, Soho Theatre and the BBC, along with regional theatres and touring companies. She works with communities, campaigns, scientists and specialists. Current work includes *Bordered* for BBC Radio 4, about human rights and the migrant crisis, a new opera *Lazarus* for Birmingham Opera, and The Centre for Alternative Technology's *Zero Carbon: Making it Happen* report. Sarah is narrative artist with Cardboard Citizens, who make theatre with and for homeless people. She teaches playwriting at Manchester University and is a Wales Green Hero.

The New Weather Institute

We are a co-operative think-tank, focused on forecasting change and making the weather. We were created to accelerate the rapid transition to a fair economy that thrives within planetary boundaries. We bring together radical thinkers, scientists, economists, makers, artists and activists to find, design and advocate ways of working and living that are more humane, reasonable and effective.

Web: www.newweather.org
Twitter: @NewWeatherInst

The Real Press

The Real Press is a small, independent publisher, specialising in history books with an edge, a description broad enough to include this one.

Web: www.therealpress.co.uk
Twitter: @therealpresspub